J. Fitzgerald (Joseph Fitzgerald) Molloy

The Life and Adventures of Edmund Kean

Vol. I

J. Fitzgerald (Joseph Fitzgerald) Molloy

The Life and Adventures of Edmund Kean
Vol. I

ISBN/EAN: 9783337177706

Printed in Europe, USA, Canada, Australia, Japan

Cover: Foto ©Raphael Reischuk / pixelio.de

More available books at **www.hansebooks.com**

THE LIFE AND ADVENTURES

OF

EDMUND KEAN

TRAGEDIAN.

1787—1833.

BY

J. FITZGERALD MOLLOY,

AUTHOR OF

"THE LIFE AND ADVENTURES OF PEG WOFFINGTON";
"COURT LIFE BELOW STAIRS, OR LONDON UNDER THE GEORGES";
"ROYALTY RESTORED, OR LONDON UNDER CHARLES II.";
"FAMOUS PLAYS," &c.

IN TWO VOLUMES.

VOL. I.

London:

WARD AND DOWNEY,

12, YORK STREET, COVENT GARDEN, W.C.

1888.

PREFACE.

In the following pages an attempt is made to present EDMUND KEAN as the central figure of a picture, surrounded by a group of players familiar to the town in the early decades of this century. The story of his strange and changeful career must alike interest lovers of the drama and students of humanity. Neither does comedy contain circumstances more varied, nor tragedy present incidents more pathetic, than those he experienced in his brief life and untimely death. His vivid imagination, clear perception, and uncommon sensibility endowed him with extraordinary powers, and at the same time subjected him to baleful influences from which his less gifted and more happy fellows were free; so that he was not less remarkable for his success than notable for his misfortune.

In writing these volumes, on which neither time nor trouble has been spared, I have been greatly helped by notes found amongst papers of the late Mr. John Forster, who, as Charles Lamb states, was at work upon

*

the tragedian's life.   Likewise am I indebted to Mr. Henry Irving, who has kindly placed at my disposal a most rare and valuable collection of Kean's portraits, play-bills in which his name appears, newspaper cuttings relating to his public and private career, criticisms on his performances, together with some original letters. Mr. Morrison's courtesy has also enabled me to print for the first time some interesting letters of this actor; whilst some valuable information from the rich resources of biographical lore stored in the library of the British Museum has been brought to light.

Contemporary players, a goodly group in all, whose achievements or failures form chapters in the annals of the Stage, have been introduced as standards whereby Edmund Kean's mental and moral height and bearing may be measured and contrasted.   That the history of these also as set down here may afford attraction and diversion is the earnest hope of the Author.

CONTENTS OF VOLUME I.

CHAPTER I.

CHAPTER II.

CHAPTER V.

CHAPTER VI.

CHAPTER VII.

CHAPTER VIII.

CHAPTER IX.

EDMUND KEAN.

EDMUND KEAN.

CHAPTER I.

Birth of Edmund Kean—A remarkable pedigree—The facetious Mr. Carey—Moses Kean the mimic—Edmund Kean the elder—His unhappy fate—A strange ordeal—A tragic incident—The opening of Drury Lane Theatre—John Kemble and Mrs. Siddons—Young Kean's engagements—His first appearance in tragedy—Runs away to sea—A clever performance—Charles Young's remembrance of Kean—Kindly Mrs. Clarke—A youthful player—Acting Richard III.—A new life and its ending—Departure and return—His bed of roses.

TOWARDS four o'clock one bleak and bitter morning in the month of March, 1787, Miss Tidswell, a player engaged at Drury Lane, was wakened by the sound of loud rapping at the street door of the house in which she dwelt. Rising hurriedly, and opening the window of her bedroom to inquire the cause of this disturbance, she was greeted by a voice she recognized as that of Edmund Kean. Lifting his head, he spoke to her in a tone at once of confidence and entreaty, saying, " Nance Carey is with child, and begs you will go to her at her lodgings in Chancery Lane."

Soon Miss Tidswell and her aunt Mrs. Byrne, muffled against the chill atmosphere, were, accompanied by Kean, treading their way through streets silent save for the echo of their footsteps, the watchman's drowsy cry, or the sound of belfry clocks chiming the passing quarters above the sleeping world ; and dark but for the yellow flames of oil lamps burning dimly at odd corners, or suspended above the arched entrances of courts and alleys. Arriving at the poor and wretched apartment where the suffering woman lay, her friends asked if she had made the necessary preparations for the child who was about to be born. With an air of indifference, she replied she had not. Therefore Mrs. Byrne, a good-natured Irish woman, florid of face and rotund of person, given to many words and charitable deeds, expressed surprise, and presently went to bor-row some baby clothes from friendly neighbours. And Nance Carey's room being comfortless, chill, and dreary, she was moved to her father's chambers close by in Gray's Inn, where soon after a male child was born, who was called Edmund Kean, and subsequently known as England's greatest tragic actor.

The infant's pedigree on both sides was somewhat remarkable. Nance Carey had come of a family well known in the world of art. Her grandfather, Henry Carey, was a natural son of George Saville, Marquis of Halifax, a patron of genius, one likewise who laid claim to literary honours. Henry Carey was famous as a composer of songs, a musician of some merit, a writer for the stage, and the supposed author of the National Anthem. As the composer of *Sally in our Alley*, which Addison praised for its words, and Geminiani lauded for its harmony, his memory abides with us. Moreover has his name been blessed by many as the original projector of the fund for decayed musicians. His songs were sung by high and low; his farces gained considerable success; and his humour was well appreciated, inasmuch as his generation styled him "the facetious Mr. Carey." One of his dramatic pieces, produced in the year 1715, bore the remarkable title, *Marriage and Hanging*. Strange to narrate, he experienced both ordeals. He married, and became the father of a son named after the Marquis, George Saville. In the course of time, years weighed heavily on Henry Carey. Misfortune had quenched his humour, poverty had killed his wit, hunger gnawed his vitals, the world became black to his sight. So it

happened one gray October afternoon that his wife,
entering the chill and cheerless garret of a house in
Warwick Street, Coldbath Fields, where they lodged,
beheld her husband's body suspended from the rafters
by a rope round his neck, his gray head sunk upon his
breast, his eyes wide open and aglare, his nerveless
limbs hanging motionless from their trunk.

George Saville Carey, the father of Nance, and
grandfather of Edmund Kean, had been bred a printer,
but became a player. His histrionic talents were not
considerable, and at the end of his first season at
Covent Garden Theatre he was not re-engaged. However, he was a man of various talents and divers
resources, destined to play many parts in his brief day.
That he might earn bread, he delivered lectures in the
principal towns of England on mimicry, a talent for
which he was remarkable. Subsequently he wrote a
ballad opera, an interlude, a burlesque, a burletta, a
masque, a comedy, and several songs, some of which
are now attributed to Dibdin. But all his efforts to
court the smiles of Fortune were vain; success escaped
him, pursue her as he would. From youth to age his
life was one of continued hardship and bitter struggle;
nor did the conduct of his daughter help to lighten his
burden.

At the age of fifteen, she left his home to join a company of players, who sought favour in the provinces. As an actress she showed slight talent, and her services were not in constant demand. Her brother played the guitar, sang, and recited, and with her aid gave entertainments in the suburbs. In person she was not unattractive; her eyes were large and dark, her features comely, her figure shapely. In the course of time she engaged the attention of Edmund Kean, the youngest of a family of three brothers of Irish descent, who lived at No. 9 St. Martin's Lane, where a widowed sister, Mrs. Price, kept house for them.

The elder brothers were named Aaron and Moses. The first was remarkable for nothing in particular, save his love for drink; Moses, on the contrary, was a notable character, who earned his bread as a tailor and a mimic. According to his advertisements, "he delineated with perspicuity the voices, gestures, and manners of the most conspicuous characters of the Senate and the Stage." He was at once realistic and comical; no mimicry so excellent had been witnessed since the days of Samuel Foote; like him, Moses also possessed a vein of satire and a wooden leg. For years he had a regular summer engagement at the Haymarket Theatre, where in days of yore Foote had drawn goodly crowds

to behold their neighbours' weaknesses held up to merry
sport and diverting ridicule. The spirit of brotherly
love and Christian charity which animated the public
in the days of Samuel Foote was not less strong in
those of Moses Kean. He became a favourite with
the town, and such was his popularity, that his audiences invariably began to applaud when they heard
the stumping of his wooden leg behind the scenes.
Their faithfulness to him was proved on one occasion,
when a rival mimic named Rees undertook to burlesque Moses in an interlude, called *Thimble's flight
from the Shopboard.* This piece was intended to be
produced between two plays at the Haymarket Theatre;
but when Rees came upon the stage, the whole house
rose and hissed him off the boards.

Moses was not only popular inside the theatre, but
well liked throughout the town. His appearance and
dress rendered him readily distinguishable. A stout-
built man with black bushy hair, he dressed in a scarlet
coat, white satin waistcoat, black satin breeches, and
bright blue stockings; a long-quartered shoe with a
great buckle covered his foot, and a cocked hat adorned
his head. His humour was well appreciated by his
companions, and he possessed the reputation of being a
wag. Once while under examination in the Court of

King's Bench, Garrow the solicitor said in solemn tones, "You are, I believe, an imitator, are you not?" "So they tell me," replied Moses, in tones of comic pathos. "Tell you," said the solicitor sturdily; "you know it. Are you not in the habit of taking people off?" "Oh, yes," he replied, "and I shall take myself off the moment you have done with me."

Edmund Kean was unlike his brothers in appearance, being remarkably handsome in face and graceful in figure. Quite early in life his abilities as an orator were recognized, and he was known as a fluent speaker at the debating societies at that time in vogue, from those at the Lyceum and Coachmakers' Hall, to the free-and-easy clubs held at taverns. Moreover, he occasionally assisted his brother Moses in his entertainments. At the date when his acquaintance with Nance Carey began he was clerk to an architect named Wilmot, who was then building the Royalty Theatre. His intimacy with her brought him no good, for the evil fortune which had attended her family seemed to attach itself to him. From being a youth of promise, he fell into evil ways, drank heavily, and lost his clerkship. Gradually he grew reduced in circumstances, but was at length received in the office of Mr. Lush of Charles Square as a copying clerk. The habit he had contracted unfortunately continued; he still drank, became impoverished, gloomy, and despondent, and finally went mad.

The history of his remaining days is pathetic and tragic. His madness was of that order which did not require restraint, nor yet give ground for hope. His life was passed in melancholy and silence; the world had become for him blank as an ocean on which darkness has fallen; existence was a vast waste where day and night were one, and time was all unknown. With the passage of months a change came over the saddened household in St. Martin's Lane, for the rough cheery voice of Moses was no longer heard ringing through its familiar rooms; no more did the well-known stumping of his wooden leg sound upon the stair. He who had brought bread to the household was taken, and he was left who was its care. And as Moses, no longer clad in those garments of glowing colours which had been his pride, but decently wrapped in shroud cloths, lay white-faced and fixed in his coffin, it was hoped that if his insane brother was brought to his side, some memory within him might move the frozen current of his mind, and reason, long congealed, mayhap return once more. The experiment was weird, ghastly, and solemn.

Accordingly, he from whom reason had fled whilst yet his years were young, sad-eyed, pale, and speechless, was brought into the room chilled and darkened by death, and led to where the yellow light of candles fell upon the closed eyelids and sunken features of the dead, and on the form rigid beneath its folded drapery. At first the hushed and sombre apartment and its silent tenant had no perceptible effect upon this witless visitor; but gradually his vacant eyes fastened upon the features of his brother, a new light crept into them, a troubled expression flashed across his face, tears slowly fell upon his cheeks, and when his glance met the anxious gaze of those beside him, they saw with infinite relief and heartfelt gratitude that reason had returned.

This change did not, however, continue long; for again his mind lost its balance, and he became more restless and excited than before. And it happened one day that, getting on the roof of the house, he walked along the parapet, when either accidentally losing his footing, or purposely jumping from the height, he fell into the street beneath. When those nearest approached him he was dead.

Meanwhile his child, born into poverty, met with neglect. Nance Carey, who never betrayed either care or affection for her son, nursed him for three months,

and then declining to be furthermore troubled with
him, she left him in the care of his father, and set out
to join a company of strolling players. Edmund Kean,
at this time in his right mind, placed the child in charge
of a nurse, who, probably not being paid for her services,
neglected the infant, so that his legs became almost
deformed, and were subsequently only brought to their
proper shape by the use of irons. When he was about
four years old his mother returned to town from her
wanderings and claimed the lad, believing she could
reap some paltry profit from his appearance on the
stage. Accordingly, when Nouverre's ballet-opera of
Cymon was about to be produced at Drury Lane
Theatre, little Edmund Carey, as he was then called,
was, amongst other children, a candidate for the part of
Cupid. His fine dark eyes, his "little gestures," and his
anxiety to be chosen, recommended him to the stage
manager, who selected him to represent the god of love
destined to sit at the feet of Sylvia and Cymon in an
enchanted car. His representation was a success, and
by way of reward, he was presently engaged to represent demons, apes, and fairies in pantomimes. At the
age of six he made a memorable appearance on the stage.

The occasion was one of unusual importance. On
the 4th of June, 1791, Drury Lane Theatre, sacred to

the shades of Wilkes, Booth, and Cibber; Bracegirdle, Woffington, and Clive; Quin, Macklin, and Garrick, was closed for rebuilding. It had been erected one hundred and seventeen years, been several times altered and repaired, and now required thorough reconstruction. Two years later a new house had risen on its site, enlarged in size, commodious in its resources, handsome in its ornamentation. The accommodations for the stage were on a more extensive scale than those of any other house in Europe at that date. A large ventilator admitted fresh air; four great reservoirs, from which water could be conveyed to any part of the house in case of fire, were built above the roof; a fire-proof iron curtain was constructed, which in case of need was supposed to prevent flames breaking out on the stage from reaching the auditorium. Moreover the ceiling was handsomely painted, and the fronts of the boxes decorated by Italian artists; chandeliers of crystal and silver lighted the house, and the pillars supporting the stage were inlaid with mirrors.

On the 13th of March, 1793, an audience assembled for the first time in the new theatre to hear a concert of sacred music; and eight days later the first dramatic performance was given here. The play selected for the occasion was *Macbeth*, which John Philip Kemble undertook to produce with unusual care and splendour, and such novelty as might consist in some departures from the customary manner of presenting the tragedy. The scenery was new, handsome, and appropriate; the witches no longer wore mittens, plaited caps, laced aprons, red stomachers, and ruffs such as they had adorned themselves withal when Garrick played Macbeth in a modern court suit and a bag wig. They now were habited in robes appropriate to their state and circumstance; glittering serpents coiled themselves round their bodies; black spirits and white, blue spirits and gray, attended them; the visible presence of Banquo was omitted from the banquet scene.

John Philip Kemble played the murderous Thane; his sister, Mrs. Siddons, Lady Macbeth; whilst their brother, Charles Kemble, made his first appearance in London as Malcolm, and was audibly derided during his performance. A prologue was spoken by the manager, and an epilogue by Miss Farren, in which she assured her hearers they need have no fear of fire, as there was water enough at hand to drown them all— at which words the curtain rose, and a river was seen in which a waterman in his boat rowed himself to and fro; likewise she referred to the iron curtain, which would prevent all from being burned save the scenes and the actors.   At the conclusion a view of Shakespeare's monument, under a mulberry tree, was exhibited, and *The Mulberry Tree*, and *Where the bee Sucks*, were sung, much to the satisfaction of all.

Now little Edmund Carey, amongst a crowd of other lads, represented an attendant spirit on the sisters three. His personation was, however, limited to a single night, for whilst he and his fellow-demons stood in a row one before the other at the mouth of a cave, preparatory to scampering round the cauldron, he either accidentally or intentionally made a forward step which he was unable to recover.   He therefore fell against the demon in front of him, who in turn knocked down his next neighbour, and he doing likewise, they tumbled one upon the other until the whole wicked company lay prostrate.   Confusion followed this unrehearsed action; the audience tittered, and the scene was spoiled. Hippen, who narrates the anecdote, says Kemble regarded the occurrence as a breach of discipline.   At the conclusion of the act the chief offender was brought before him, and little Carey answered his reproaches by merely remarking, "This was the first time he had performed in tragedy."

Henceforth *Macbeth* was played without the representatives of the powers of darkness; but this misadventure did not prevent Edmund Carey from being engaged to play imps and apes as before during the pantomime season. His connection with the theatre was chiefly owing to Miss Tidswell, a tall, handsome woman, who had been introduced by the Duke of Norfolk to David Garrick, who secured for her an engagement to play petty parts in Drury Lane Theatre, a position she still maintained. His Grace is remembered in history for having at the Whig Club drank a toast, "To the majesty of the people," hearing of which action poor George III., at this time supposed by courtesy to be in the enjoyment of sanity, with his own right royal hand erased the duke's name from the Privy Council list. Because of the Duke of Norfolk's interest in Miss Tidswell, Kean when he grew up felt inclined to believe they were his parents ; but of this supposition he was eventually thoroughly dissuaded.

Miss Tidswell behaved to the lad with a kindness his mother never extended towards him. She it was who took him with her to the theatre, where he stood during the performances at the wings, his dark eyes full of wonderment and admiration, his ears drinking in speeches which he would presently delight the supernumeraries by repeating in the same tone and with the same gestures as he had heard and seen. She it was who in her own rooms taught him to recite, and through her interference was he sent to school. But the school-room was, alas! a place he abhorred; constraint was irksome to his nature; his tasks were ignored, and he rebelled against punishment. Finally he determined to escape from thraldom. Possibly he had read of the sea, and heroes that sail thereon, until his vivid imagination pictured the wonderful adventures that might take him from his abominated surroundings and place him in a world brightened by the splendour of romance. So it happened one day he announced to his mother that he wished to be a sailor, whereon she thrashed him soundly by way of banishing such nonsense from his brain.

His punishment had not the desired effect. A self-contained lad of ten years, accustomed to think and act for himself at a time when other boys merely obey the wishes of their elders, he hastened to put his resolution into action; and early one morning, before the house was astir, he crept from his mother's lodgings, taking with him his scanty belongings, and made his slow way to Portsmouth. If any efforts were exerted to capture him, they were not successful, for he soon shipped as a cabin-boy on board a vessel bound for Madeira. The voyage by no means realized his expectations; no pirate brig with sails full set, port holes bristling with cannon, and death's head flying at the mast, bore down upon them; nor were they stranded on coral reefs stretching from unknown islands, inhabited by a wild but friendly race. All was sordid drudgery and black misery, hunger, curses, and the rope's end, and he resolved to escape this bitter fate. The means by which he sought to avoid work wer highly ingenious in one of his age, and the manner in which they were carried out gave proof of his possessing in youth the great powers which rendered his manhood distinguished.

From exposure and wetting on the outward voyage he caught cold, which he avowed on reaching port resulted in total deafness. To the shouts of the captain or the oaths of the sailors he was apparently insensible; neither expression nor movement betrayed the slightest consciousness of the commands addressed to him, or the imprecations hurled at him. But fearing this assumption of infirmity was insufficient to gain the ends desired, he likewise feigned lameness, and declaring he had lost the use of his limbs remained in his bunk. Being no longer of service, he was carried to an hospital, where he remained a puzzle to the medical faculty, who vainly sought to discover the cause of his malady. As a last effort to restore him, they recommended he should be moved to his native country, and as his vessel was then departing he was shipped in her once more. And now was his courage and consistency severely tested; for scarce had the vessel left the port when a storm, black, fierce, and sudden, arose, threatening destruction and death. All hands on board save the invalid were at work; men who had battled through a hundred gales believed their last hour had come; but the lad, never stirring, continued to play his part bravely to the last act, which ended, not in darkness and tragedy, but in safety and gladness. And being landed at Southampton, he quickly regained the use of his limbs, and tramped to London.

Returning to his mother's lodgings in Ewer Street, Southwark, he was told she had joined Richardson's show and gone into the country; he therefore turned his face towards the residence of " Aunt Tid," as he had learned to call Miss Tidswell. She welcomed her old favourite with gladness, received him into her home, and seeing the direction in which his talents lay, read Shakespeare with him, and taught him to recite. Nay she occasionally acted scenes with him, and, as he remembered afterwards, taught him to say " Alas, poor Uncle !" instead of " Alas, poor Yorick !" when repeating

Hamlet's speech to Horatio above the new-made grave
of Ophelia, training him in this manner to throw feeling
into his voice. Occasionally his detestation even of
such mild restraint, his love for excitement and desire
for novelty,—attributes all of the genius within him,—
caused him to leave her house and wander for days
in distant suburbs, where at various taverns he recited and sang, tumbled and danced, imitated monkeys
and devils, and enjoyed brief independence ; then would
he return to Aunt Tid, rich with coins awarded him
by admiring audiences.

This pleasant period of his life was interrupted by
the return of his mother, who, foreseeing the use he
might be, claimed him once more. The next glimpse
is given of young Edmund Kean by Charles Young,
whom some in years after raised to the distinction of
Kean's rival. Charles Young's father, Thomas Young,
was an eminent physician, and an hospitable host. On
one occasion, towards Christmas, when Charles was back
from Eton for the holidays, he remembered a dinner
being given at his father's house to which some people
of distinction were bidden. He was allowed to join the
company when dessert was served, and as he descended
the stairs and passed on his way to the dining-room
through the hall, he saw seated there a slatternly

woman with a boy standing beside her, dressed in a somewhat fantastic garb, and "with the blackest and most penetrating eyes he had ever beheld in human head." He believed they were strolling gipsies from Bartholomew Fair, who had come to seek medical advice, and passed them by; but presently, when one of the servants whispered his master, the latter bade him "bring in the boy." Little Edmund Kean, for he it proved, was led in, taken by the hand, patted on the head, and requested to favour the company with a specimen of his recitations. With great self-possession he stood apart, knit his dark brows, thrust up one shoulder, and began the opening soliloquy of *Richard III*. His delivery was marked by such feeling and expression that he was greeted by warm applause; when he gave further proof of his abilities as an actor; nay, he sang songs, merry and pathetic, danced a hornpipe, and for an hour kept the company amused. Then a napkin was spread upon the floor, into which a shower of silver was flung, which was afterwards conveyed to the pockets of the lad, who, smiling and bowing gracefully, retired.

It happened one day some months later, that Mrs. Clarke of Guildford Street called on Surgeon Young's wife. Her visit having ended, she was about to leave the house, when as she passed through the hall Thomas Young opened the door of his study and said, "Pray come in, my dear lady. I have," he added, "a charming woman to introduce to you, and I know your heart will warm towards her, for she is the daughter of your favourite George Saville Carey."

As Mrs. Clarke entered the room, Young led towards her a woman whose graceful figure was clad in shabby garments set off with faded finery, and whose cheeks were coloured with rouge. Though her appearance did not at first recommend her to Mrs. Clarke, yet her respectful bearing and air of refinement appealed to her better nature.

"She is in very reduced circumstances," Young said in an explanatory tone, "and hopes you will help her."

Mrs. Clarke asked in what manner she could be of assistance; to which Young, acting as spokesman, replied, "She is obliged to sell perfumes and the like. Here, my dear," he said, addressing Nance Carey, "where is your basket? Ah, here it is—Marechale powder, Japanese pomatum, millefleurs, Hungary water, genuine *eau de Cologne*—everything a woman wants."

Mrs. Clarke bought some lavender water and departed, having first given Nance Carey permission to call occasionally at her house. Of this the seller of toilet requisites soon availed herself, and during one of her visits made mention of her wonderful little boy, who had an astonishing genius for acting. He was now being brought up very genteelly by a Roman Catholic lady; he sang in her chapel, served the altar, and "threw the incense about." Mrs. Clarke hoped he would be left under her protection, and no further remarks were made concerning him. As for herself, she acted whenever she could get engagements, and when disengaged sold her wares to earn a livelihood. Mrs. Clarke was not only a constant purchaser, but occasionally gave her cast-off articles of wearing apparel, amongst which was a "tiffany painted skirt, spangled too," with which Nance Carey was much delighted.

It came to pass that one morning in June, when Mrs. Clarke was sitting in her back drawing-room, an irregular, tremulous knock at the street door fell upon her ear, and presently Charles, an old and faithful servant, slow in pace and deliberate in words, whose hair had grown gray in the service of his mistress, appeared before her. A smile brightened his face as if his fancy were tickled.

"Master Carey, ma'am, is below," he said, "and wishes to see you."

"Master Carey!" she repeated, for the moment forgetful of his individuality.

"Yes, ma'am; he belongs to Miss Carey who brings perfumes."

"Tell him to send up his message."

"I did, ma'am; but he says he must speak to you."

"Then show him up," she said.

Charles slowly departed, but soon the drawing-room door was again thrown open, and a slender, pale-faced boy, diminutive in size, with large dark eyes and curling auburn hair, entered, and bowed with the air of a prince. His jacket and trousers were shabby almost to raggedness, his whole appearance indicated poverty and neglect. An expression of sensibility, an air of refinement, and a look of delicacy in his bearing appealed to her and touched her heart with pity. Before she could speak, he said in a self-possessed, graceful, and courteous manner—

"My mother, madam, desires her humble duty, and requests you will be so good as to advance her the loan of a shilling to take the spangled petticoat you kindly gave her out of the pawn. She would not have troubled you, but we are going to play at Islington to-night, and she has all but one shilling."

His message conveyed a history.

"Do you play also?" Mrs. Clarke asked.

"Oh yes," he replied, with the ready egotism of youth; "I can act a good many things."

"What are they?" she asked, already interested in this clever lad.

"Scenes from *Richard III.*, *Hamlet*, and *Macbeth.* Then I can play harlequin and the clown too, and sing and dance."

"I should like to see you act," she remarked.

"And I should be very happy if I might act to you," he replied.

"Then will you come to me to-morrow evening?" she asked.

"Oh yes," he answered eagerly. "What shall I do, madam?"

"What you like best."

"Then that will be *Richard III.* I must have a tent," he continued, growing excited at the prospect. "I begin with the tent scene," and he cast his eyes round the room searchingly.

Mrs. Clarke stood up, opened the folding doors, and entered the front drawing-room, in which was a bow window.

"You shall act here," she said to him.

The dark eyes blazed with delight, the poor pinched

face lighted with enthusiasm. "This bow window,"
he said, "is the very thing. I can pin the curtains
together and make a tent, and this little sofa will be
the couch. Have you a bell for me to ring, and may
I have some music before I begin?"

Mrs. Clarke said she knew a young lady who could
play the *Battle of Prague*, and she would invite her
to be present.

It was then arranged he was to come next evening
at half-past six o'clock, and having received the shilling
for his mother, he departed full of gladness. In the
course of the afternoon Mrs. Clarke called on a few
friends and neighbours, and invited them to come and
witness the performance of this marvellous boy. Next
evening they assembled in her drawing-room, and
shortly before the appointed time, the same timid,
nervous knock which she heard yesterday sounded at
the street door. Good-hearted Mrs. Clarke hastened
down to meet her little *protégé*, and survey his attire
before presenting him to her guests. He was dressed
in the same threadbare jacket and trousers, his face
had been newly washed, and a white muslin frilled
handkerchief of his mother's was tied round his neck
by way of collar.

His hostess, taking him by the hand, hastily led

him towards her dressing-room, and there took the pack-thread out of his shoes and tied them with black silk ribbons. Whilst she was engaged in this manner his quick eye, travelling round the room, caught sight of a great riding-hat with feathers, and he instantly said, "That would exactly suit Richard." Then noticing a belt and sword which had belonged to Mrs. Clarke's brother in his childhood, he cried out with boyish delight, "A real sword! Oh, dear madam, may I have a real sword?"

She replied it was intended for him, and having made some additions to his toilet, and given him the hat, sword, and belt, hand-in-hand she descended with him to the drawing-room. Then he flung himself on the sofa under the pinned curtains; the ghosts of those he had murdered were haunting Richard's dreams. The *Battle of Prague* began with many a bang; cannons roared, victims shrieked, armies advanced and retreated over the vibrating notes of the piano, and when at last peace was restored, up roused Richard, pale and scared by the sights he had seen, and spoke his speech. Before he concluded women wept. His audience had not been prepared for the energy and feeling which animated the feeble frame, and lighted the pallid face of this boy. He was greeted with loud applause, and gracious words were spoken to him. He had tasted the joys of success. The hostess then proposed that tea should be served, but he begged that he might "act the fight with Richmond."

"By yourself?" it was asked.

"Yes, you will see; I can do it very well. It was for that," he added, "I wanted the sword."

His fight created still greater astonishment, and he died with a skill and grace wonderful in one of his age.

An old gentleman present, gifted with more good nature than tact, flung a half-crown upon the mimic stage. Richard, however, did not deign to notice the act; but the example of the donor being quickly followed, a handsome sum was presented to the lad. He refused to accept it, saying the lady of the house was his mother's best friend, and he could take no money. At the request of his hostess he eventually accepted it, and having eaten cake, drank tea, and answered the questions of his admirers, he was sent home, with instructions to call next day.

His budding talents and inbred gentleness won the heart of Mrs. Clarke, a childless wife, and becoming daily more interested in this waif, she resolved to take him into her home. Cleanliness, sufficient food, and generous care created a new life for him, but nothing seemed to give him such delight as his little bed; the white cotton curtains of the crib were printed with crimson roses such as never bloomed in earthly gardens, from which fact he was wont to speak of this nest as his bed of roses. His existence was now one of perfect happiness, and no boy could behave better. The affection of his friend increased hourly. Every morning he went to school, and occasionally in the evenings he recited at the homes of Mrs. Clarke's friends, she stipulating he should be called for and sent back. For his performances he invariably received money, the greater part of which was sent to his mother, the remainder being kept for his private use.

That she might add to his greater delight, his friend frequently sent him in charge of Charles to the theatre when the Kembles acted; and on his return, Charles, who was fond of the boy, used to narrate with great glee, whilst he rubbed his hands and nodded his head, that it was better than the play to watch master Carey's face. "All the play was to be seen there." He clapped his hands louder than any one else, and was ever ready to hiss at the slightest disturbance which interfered with the performance. When in the autumn Mrs. Clarke left town, she placed little Edmund Kean in charge of a motherly old woman who lived near the school which he attended; and on her return she considered it better he should remain where he was, with the understanding that he was to see her daily, and lunch and dine with her frequently. Now a short time after her return to town she received a visit from some friends in the country. These consisted of an old-fashioned Tory gentleman, rotund in person, pompous in manner, and somewhat foolish in speech, together with his mild-mannered wife and two daughters, children of ten and twelve years.

One day during their stay little Edmund Kean had a holiday, that he might come and play with them; they were delighted with their bright-witted companion, who sang, tumbled, and acted for them. And so well did he please them, that next day he was invited to dinner, after which a visit to the play-house was contemplated. Accordingly he came, dressed in his best suit, his spirits rising high in anticipation of the pleasure before him; and as he sat at table between his two new friends, he chatted with them gaily, and spoke much of the theatre.

Once when one of them questioned him regarding *Macbeth*, which they were about to see, he gave such a clear description of the plot and situations of the tragedy, that though he spoke in an undertone, those near paused to listen, until suddenly becoming aware of the attention paid him, he stopped, blushed, and caught the eyes of the country gentleman, from whose conversation he had momentarily diverted the interest, fixed upon him with disapproving gaze.

The cloth being removed, some friendly discussion was held as to the disposal of the party in two carriages, and Edmund Kean's name being mentioned, the burly gentleman said, in accents of astonishment and indignation, "What! does *he* come with us?" Mrs. Clarke was momentarily silent from surprise, and her glance fell upon her *protégé*. With his face flushing from anger, and his eyes sparkling with indignation, he rose from the table, and slowly walked towards the door. In his passage he passed the backs of the chairs, and as he came near his hostess she caught hold of his hand, which trembled in hers, and pressing it, whispered him to ask Charles for three-and-sixpence, and go into the pit; but he merely shook his head in answer, and next instant had gone. As the hall door slammed Mrs. Clarke, with some foreboding of pain, went to the window and saw her favourite going down the street at a rapid pace, without his hat, his head erect, his whole bearing indicating wounded pride.

For her the tragedy of *Macbeth* had not much interest

that night. Instead of watching the movements of
John Philip Kemble or Mrs. Siddons, she leaned from
her box, looking in the pit for the familiar figure or
the upturned face of her little friend ; but her search
was vain.   Next day her guests departed, and Mrs.
Clarke immediately sent her maid to the boy's lodgings,
but she returned with the information that he was not
there ; the previous evening he had rushed to his room,
changed his new clothes for his old, and hurried out
again without answering a question or speaking a word.
It was then surmised that he must have gone to his
mother's, but days passed, and he failed to make his
appearance.   Mrs. Clarke, now thoroughly uneasy, sent
Charles to inquire for him, but he brought word that
Miss Carey had not seen her son for over a week.   Mrs.
Clarke was therefore seized by a fear that he had in a
moment of anger thrown himself into the Thames, or
got crushed under the wheels of carriages at the doors
of the theatre.   Search was made for him far and near,
but no trace could be found of him ; he had completely
vanished.

But it happened early in the morning of the seventh
day after his disappearance, a good-natured ostler from
the adjoining mews, who knew the lad, and liked him
well, carried his insensible form to the door of Mrs.

Clarke's house. He had found him near the door of his stable, fast asleep as he thought at first, and strove to wake him; but when the boy opened his eyes he was unconscious of where he was, and being placed on his legs he fell down again from weakness. In appearance he was travel-stained, dirty, miserable, and starved. With mingled pain and joy Mrs. Clarke beheld him once more, kissed him whilst tears blinded her eyes, and carried him to the bed in which she had often watched him peacefully sleep. There he was tended with great care and anxious love, until at last he opened his dark eyes, and his lips were seen to move. Putting her ear close above them she heard him ask, "Am I in heaven in my bed of roses?"

CHAPTER II.

WHEN the lad recovered he told his kind friend the simple story of his flight, blushing with shame that he had caused her so much anxiety. Full of anger and indignation at the slight which the country gentleman had put upon him, he resolved to leave town, and never return until he was a great man. He had walked to Bristol, and again offered himself as a sailor, but he was so pale and thin no captain would hire him. So tired and hungry was he that he could neither recite nor sing, and ask for bread he would not. He therefore came back to town, resolved to die near the house of the friend who loved him. It was night when he arrived, and the stables were the best shelter he could find. He remembered no more.

After some days spent in consideration and consultation with her friends, Mrs. Clarke came to the conclusion he had better be placed under the care of some one able to exercise more control over him than she possessed; and believing he would never follow any other calling than that of an actor, she waited on Miss de Champ, a clever actress, who subsequently became Mrs. Charles Kemble, to have her opinion regarding him. Miss de Champ remembered him well, and narrated, that one morning before rehearsal began at the theatre, she was crossing the stage, when sounds of loud applause arrested her attention. Inquiring its cause, she was told it was only little Kean acting Richard III. " I went into the green-room," she said, "and saw the little fellow facing an admiring group, and reciting lustily, and in my opinion he was very clever." She was afraid, however, no opening could be found for him at Drury Lane Theatre, for he had drawn upon himself the anger of John Philip Kemble, who on another occasion during rehearsal caught the lad mimicking him, to the great amusement of the

underlings of the theatre. Kemble had surprised him,
and being angry, pushed him aside so roughly that
he fell through a trap-door, and was lamed for some
time. Another man of wider mind and more generous
instincts than Kemble, seeing the lad's genius, would
have trained and educated him for the stage, but he
never extended a helping hand to the boy who was
destined to cast him from the position of first English
tragedian, which he had held so long.

A few days after her conversation with Miss de
Champ, Mrs. Clarke received a visit from Captain
Miller of the Staffordshire Militia, then on duty at
Windsor Castle. To him she confided her perplexity,
and asked his advice regarding Kean, who was now in
his twelfth year. After some conversation, Captain
Miller offered to take the lad with him to Windsor, a
proposition to which Mrs. Clarke assented. It was
arranged that before his departure he should give an
evening's entertainment in public, that he might raise
funds sufficient to start him in the world. A room was
accordingly taken in Chancery Lane, a programme
arranged, and tickets printed. The performance was
to be given solely by himself, an undertaking from
which a man of experience might have shrank ; but
his courage and exertions were amply rewarded, as

his receipts amounted to between forty and fifty pounds.

Captain Miller lodged him at the barracks, where he speedily drew attention by his mimicry, acting, tumbling, and singing. So bright and clever a boy had never been seen, and the officers found in him a source of infinite entertainment. Presently his fame spread to Eton, where he was introduced to some of the elder boys, and to the royal household, when George III. expressed himself anxious to see this phenomenon. This was an honour he had not hoped to receive. Twice he recited before the king, queen, and princess, for which His Majesty, who was not remarkable for his liberality, gave him a guinea. Having stayed some time at Windsor, he went to Oxford, bearing with him a letter of introduction from an Eton boy to his elder brother then at the university; and here his success was equally satisfactory. He was *fêted* and applauded by the undergraduates, one of whom, named Conybeare, gave him the first copy of Shakespeare's plays he ever possessed.

Leaving Oxford, he returned once more to town. His mother had again joined a strolling company, and he took refuge with Aunt Tid, who resumed her instructions, and read Shakespeare with him from his own copy. By her advice he now studied, not only certain speeches and scenes, but the whole parts set down to Romeo, Hamlet, and Richard III.; and once, by her entreaties, John Kemble so far forgot the lad's offence as to let him act Arthur in *King John*, Kemble playing the King, and Mrs. Siddons Constance on this memorable occasion. Acting became more than ever the delight of his life; now we find him in the garret of a bookseller named Roach, who dwelt in a court close by Brydges Street, playing Richard III. to the Lady Anne of a Scotch lassie, who afterwards, as Mrs. Robertson, gained credit in the provinces as an actress. Her strong accent was a source of grievance to Kean, who taught her English, and in return learned from her the dialect of Sir Pertinax Macsycophant, a character he played at Drury Lane after many years had passed. Again, in the back parlour of his aunt, Mrs. Price, a dressmaker, he enacted Richard to the Richmond of Master Rae, a companion he was destined to meet with years later.

But his love of admiration and longing for excitement again seizing him, he left Miss Tidswell's home, and hired himself to Richardson, the famous showman. Richardson's show was seen at every fair within a hundred miles radius of the capital. Outside its highly coloured "wooden walls," on a platform gained by a rickety flight of steps, drums beat, fiddles squeaked, and horns sounded, keeping silence only whilst some stentorian voice shouted alluring descriptions of the wonders to be witnessed within, and heartily invited all lovers of the marvellous to step inside and secure their places. The manager was a tall man with a red face, dressed in high boots, crimson vest, and a many buttoned green coat. The fair members of his company, whose smiles sought to hide their lassitude, were decked with glazed calico, muslin flowers, tarnished tinsel, spangles and tinfoil, stockings with clocks, and shoes that had lost all shape from long service. Their cheeks were rouged, their necks adorned with mock jewellery, feathers once gay were stuck in their tousled hair. The gentlemen of the troop, fellows of infinite experience, good at turning a somersault, enacting a tragedy, cracking a whip, or beating a drum, were clad in tights and vests. The manager's receipts generally averaged forty pounds a day during the three days which a fair usually lasted; so that he was enabled to pay his first-rate tragic actors and actresses ten and sixpence a day; to "paraders or pluck in men," or ladies who were styled "aggravators," he gave seven and sixpence a day; good-looking automatons of either sex had six shillings,

whilst "underlings that neither look nor speak'
received four shillings.

Wherever the show went, bustle, noise, and merriment
travelled in its wake. On the village green, the fair,
or beside the racecourse, it was surrounded by rival
booths, the habitations of dwarfs, mermaids, and pigs
showing complete knowledge of the alphabet, of
speaking fish, two-headed boys, fat women, and strong
men. In its atmosphere dwelt confusion begotten of
the mingled strains of bag-pipes and French horns,
trumpets and fifes, the voices of fruit vendors, the
report of musketry from shooting-galleries, shrill cries
of Punch, cheers from merry-go-rounds and ups-and-
downs, roars from performing bears, choruses from the
tap-houses, shouts from the ballad-mongers, and cries
from struggling crowds.

Life in a show-box to a lad of young Kean's temperament had for a time a vast attraction. Here his songs
and recitations, his acting and tumbling, were received
with rapturous applause by ever-varying audiences.
After a while he transferred his services from Richardson's show to Saunders's circus, where he learned to
ride with great skill and grace. Here horsemanship,
tightrope-walking, and acrobatic feats were the order
of the day. A writer who contributed an article to

the *New Monthly Magazine* on the early days of Edmund Kean, remembered hearing Davies, once manager of Astley's amphitheatre, describe the occasion in which he first saw him. Considering the circumstances could not be more vividly described than in Davies's language, the author jotted down the ex-manager's phrases in his note-book.

"I was passing," he said, "down Great Surrey Street one morning, when just as I had comed to the place where the Riding House now stands at the corner of the 'Syleum, or Mag-dallen, as they calls it, I seed Master Saunders a-packing up his traps. His booth, you see, had been there standing for three or four days, or thereabouts; and on the boards in front of the painting—the prossenium, as the painter says—I seed a slim young chap with marks of paint—and bad paint it was, for all the world like ruddle on the jaw of a sheep— on his face, a-tying up some of the canwass wot the wonderfullest carakters and curosties of that 'ere exhibition was painted upon. And so when I had shook hands with Master Saunders, and all that 'ere, he turns him right round to the young chap wot had just throwd a summerset behind his back, and says, 'I say you, Master King Dick, if you don't mind what you're arter, and pack up that 'ere wan pretty tight and nimble, we shan't be off before to-morrow, that we shan't; and so you mind your eye, my lad.'"

During his engagement with Saunders the courage he showed whilst riding "fiery untamed steeds" and the daring he evinced in tumbling were notable; but once it happened that whilst attempting some unusual feat, he fell from a great height and broke his legs. As a result of this accident he suffered through life from a swelling of his instep-bones. When able he returned to Miss Tidswell, and resolved to abandon all acrobatic performances in favour of the drama. He was yet over-young and inexperienced to gain an engagement in one of the few London theatres—a consummation seldom attained save by those selected from provincial companies because of their marked abilities. His talents as a public reciter gained him prominence at the Crown and Anchor in Leicester Square, and at the Rolls Rooms in Chancery Lane, places of entertainment which were the forerunners of our modern music-halls. On the stage of the Rolls Rooms he on one occasion read the whole of the *Merchant of Venice*. Likewise, to his great delight, he played the principal parts in tragedies and comedies, acted in a private theatre in Lamb's Conduit Street. Cobham, a well-known actor in his day, who was present at some of these performances, says Kean " was the best amateur then extant."

His connection with Drury Lane playhouse, behind the scenes of which he went when he pleased, together with his familiarity with other places of entertainment, threw him continually into the company of actors, singers, and composers, who delighted in the lad's quickness and ability. From his association with Charles Incledon, who described himself as " England's greatest singer," he picked up some knowledge of music, and learned to sing correctly; D'Egville, the dancing-master, gave him at odd times lessons in his art; and from watching the fencing-master Angelo and his pupils he could soon handle the foils with dexterity, Of these men Kean in after years was wont to narrate many anecdotes. He remembered walking early one morning in the suburbs at the Surrey side of the water, when he saw Denham, a skilled musician and charming composer, whose dissipation frequently reduced him to want, stretched upon a form outside a tavern. On this hard bed the unfortunate man had lain all night, being expelled from the tap-room. Kean approached and roused him, when Denham, not yet recovered from the effect of his carousal, sat up and began strumming his fingers upon his knees. Suddenly he asked his young friend if he had got any money about him, and on receiving a reply in the affirmative, requested him to buy a sheet of paper, and bring him a ruler, together with a pen and ink. When these were set before him he quickly began to work, using the form as a desk, and soon produced a composition which seemed to have occupied his mind, set to a paraphrase of the Lord's Prayer. Handing Kean the smeared manuscripts, written with a trembling hand, he begged he would take them to some music publisher, and get what he could in exchange. Without hope of being able to dispose of them, the lad carried the sheets away, and going to Williams's of Paternoster Row, offered them to the manager. The latter at first regarded the scroll with indifference, but on a closer examination consented to try it over, and eventually handing Kean a guinea, bade him take it to the composer.

The applause which Kean received from the audiences of the Lamb's Conduit Street Theatre and the Rolls Rooms made him anxious to begin life as a player— a career which he had earnest desires and strong hopes would speedily lead him to fame and fortune. Accordingly, with the consent and by the advice of Aunt Tid, he joined the travelling company of a provincial manager; the country being the school then, as now, in which all who covet permanent distinction and not ephemeral notoriety must graduate; for labour strengthens genius as a crucible purifies gold.

The company he joined was in those days known as a commonwealth. The varied fortunes of the troop rendering stipulated salaries impossible, the receipts taken at the doors were at the end of every week divided amongst the members, according to the respective parts they played, the manager appropriating additional shares in consideration of his defraying the expenses of rent, rushlights, wardrobes, and incidental charges. Frequently the poor strollers played to empty benches, and the pittance received for their labours being small, hunger and cold afflicted them sorely. Kean, in the days when all men lauded him, and fortune's gifts were his, looking back half sadly, half wistfully on the times of bitter hardship and pitiless privation, used to narrate his experiences of a Passion week he had spent at Croydon. The theatre was closed until Easter Monday, when additional attractions were temptingly offered to the public; but meanwhile the poor players were expected to live on air, and survive, that they might fulfil the promises which the bills set forth.

Neither Kean nor the comrade who shared the expenses of his lodgings possessed a penny, the

remainder of the company were well-nigh equally impoverished, and credit was not to be expected by needy
strollers. For two days Kean, like many another genius
whom the world has known, starved; the while he
sought to strangle pangs of hunger by tightening his
waistband, and to defy depression by assuming mirth.
But the third day bringing no relief, he sought to
obtain food by strategy. Frequently had he noticed
with longing eyes a butcher's shop well-stocked and
prosperous, over which usually presided a damsel whose
buxom figure and blooming face were fair to see. To
her he resolved on addressing himself, trusting he might
obtain for love that which he had no means to buy.
Accordingly he sallied forth, and passed the shop of
which the butcher's lovely daughter was then in charge.
Her elbow rested on a round of beef, tender as the
cheek which her right hand supported; and the attitude
being one generally accepted as indicative of senti-
mentality, he hoped the hour was propitious. He
therefore advanced, but as he was about to address her,
the burly butcher came in sight, and the young tragedian passed the shop, converting the sigh which rose
for his disappointment into a whistle he trusted would
seem expressive of indifference. But presently returning,
he found the maiden all alone, when he expressed his

admiration for her charms, and gradually made known his hunger. From the round of beef which yet bore the impression of her shapely elbow she cut some solid steaks, and putting them on a skewer gave them to him. He thrust them into the tail pocket of a skirted coat, and bidding her a hasty adieu, strode homewards, rejoicing that want was at an end. But his hopes were destined to meet disappointment; for the butcher's dog, that had followed him unseen, suddenly snapped at the coat-tails, displaced the steaks, and ran off with them before Kean could recover his surprise. Surely his darkest hour had come, but dawn was at hand; for on reaching his lodging he found the London coach had brought a parcel of clothes from Aunt Tid, and as he required food rather than raiment, he hastily transferred them to the charge of his uncle, and so averted threatened starvation.

The while he struggled in the provinces he did not neglect his education; his constant practice with the foils rendered him an accomplished fencer; he read and studied Shakespeare continually, and when playing at Hodderdan in Hertfordshire, borrowed Latin and Greek dictionaries from Miss Sands, then proprietress of a public library. It was probably in this manner he gained the smattering of these languages which in after

days he was so fond of quoting. It has been stated
with much plausibility, but without a shadow of founda-
tion, that Dr. Drury, the head master of Harrow, aware
of his talents, was instrumental in sending him to Eton
for two years. Nay, the studies he pursued, his devotion
to Cicero, the Latin ode he composed and recited
whilst at Eton, have been mentioned by one who has
written his biography.   These statements, however, are
purely imaginary. A few months after his death a
controversy was carried on in the pages of *Frazer's
Magazine* as to whether he had or had not been an
Eton scholar, the question being finally settled by Dr.
Keate, who stated that the records of admission to the
school had been regularly kept since 1792; and on
examination of these, Kean's name had not been found.
He adds, he "did not believe Mr. Kean was ever a
member of that school, and he has never heard a different opinion maintained by any one connected with
the school who was likely to have accurate information."   Not these statements alone, but Kean's letters,
abounding as they do in bad grammar, would be sufficient to indicate his lack of education.

He had passed his sixteenth year when he joined
a regular theatrical company, and he remained in the
provinces for four years. Sense of freedom, hope of

adventure, good comradeship, continual excitement, to a temperament like his compensated for a life full of uncertainty and hardship. A born Bohemian, hope lit the darkness of his path, ambition beckoned him forward, love of art atoned for privations, so that he was far from being unhappy. Nay, he was wont to declare that in those days, when he received ten shillings a week as a reward for his performances in tragedy, comedy, and pantomime, he was far more content than when his salary was fifty pounds a night, and his name was praised by all men. Wise indeed are they who recognize the hour of their felicity and enjoy its pleasures; only when they have travelled up the rugged hill of life, and paused to look backward on the pathway they have trod, do men behold with regretful sight the green places they have passed and left behind for ever.

It is notable, that throughout his varied career Kean seemed conscious of the power within him, which one day would force recognition from the world. This belief helped him to labour in the hard school of experience, which was alone capable of training his talents. An anecdote which is related of him shows the estimate in which he held himself. One night as he, whilst representing Alexander the Great, was being drawn in a triumphal car before the footlights, a young fop in a stage box exclaimed, in tones loud enough to be heard by the audience, "Alexander the Great indeed! it should be Alexander the Little." The laugh into which the house would probably have broken was checked by a look which Kean deliberately and scornfully fixed upon the speaker as he rose and said, "Yes, Alexander the Little, but with a great soul;" on which all present broke into a storm of applause by way of protest against the fop's insolence and approbation of the player's spirit.

At the end of his fourth year in the provinces he applied for an engagement to Colman, Winston, and Morris, managers of the Haymarket, and his services were accepted to play small parts at a salary of two pounds a week. To London he therefore came in July, 1806.

The earlier months of this year had witnessed an event unprecedented before or after in the history of the drama, and as such must be-mentioned here. This was the appearance on the London stage of Master Betty, sometimes called the infant Roscius. His brief bright career was indeed most notable. This lad, who was born in 1791, was the son of a Belfast gentleman of property, and of a Shropshire heiress.

Passionately fond of witnessing plays and reciting poems, this lady imparted to her son the talents which subsequently rendered him remarkable. Before he was able to read he had learned to recite, committed Shakespearian speeches to memory, and accompanied their delivery with appropriate action. For the benefit and amusement of friends, the infant prodigy was frequently lifted. on a sideboard, and there declaimed to his own satisfaction and his parents' delight. As he grew up no pains were spared to train the gifts he possessed; his mother taught him elocution, his father instructed him in fencing. Recitation became a passion with him, until at last his parents, fearing it would lead him to think of a theatrical career, suddenly discountenanced what they had previously encouraged. Play-books and poems were banished, declamations interdicted, elocution lessons discontinued, and finally he was sent to school.

Here, however, Master Betty's inclinations were wakened to fresh activity by the appreciation his talents received from his companions. Towards midnight, whilst professors and teachers were enjoying the sleep of the just, the pupils' dormitory was in a state of activity and commotion. Candles smuggled into the establishment by cunning contrivances were taken from their hiding-places and lighted; beds placed side by side formed a stage; sheets were converted into classic garments, and counterpanes into curtains. Then did the hero of the night enact scenes from tragedies, recite pathetic tales and stirring ballads to an audience attired in night-shirts, who overwhelmed him with the choicest gifts in their possession—apples, peg-tops, and cakes.

It happened during his summer vacation in the year 1802, the great Mrs.. Siddons visited the Belfast Theatre. Her name was a power in the land, her fame at its highest pitch. Accompanied by their son, Mr. and Mrs. Betty witnessed her performance as Elvira in *Pizarro*. The effect on the boy was greater than they had anticipated. His face pallid from excitement, his eyes sparkling with delight, he followed the tragedy, real to him because of the genius which gave it life, force, colour. It was the first play he had seen, and the fascination which great acting exercises over the imagination, the power with which it sways the feelings, dawned on him with wonder and joy. To him the world was never the same again. After a sleepless night he rose hastily, and going out, bought a copy of *Pizarro*. Before evening he had committed Elvira's speeches to memory, and recited them after the manner of Mrs. Siddons. His usual occupations and amusements were neglected in the passion which absorbed him; by day and by night he spoke of nothing but the stage, and finally he assured his parents he should die if they would not permit him to become a player.

Though grieved by his infatuation, they were reluctant to thwart their only child, fearing their opposition to his desire might injure his health. To humour him, therefore, his father, that he might have the opinion of a competent judge, took him to Atkins, manager of the Belfast Theatre. Before him Master Betty, then in his eleventh year, recited some speeches with such effect that the manager declared "he had never indulged in the hope of seeing another Garrick, but that he had beheld an infant Garrick in Master Betty." This opinion raised the boy's hopes to a high pitch, for surely his father would not now oppose his wish to become an actor.

Soon after this consultation Ireland was again steeped in political trouble. The rebellion four years previously had drenched the land in blood, and its disastrous effects were still felt. Another rise was anticipated; clouds of fear, gloom, and grief darkened the country; martial law was proclaimed, and the theatres closed. But during the succeeding year the political atmosphere cleared, and playhouses were once more permitted to open their doors. Now Atkins, knowing that in a period of general depression some extraordinary novelty was necessary to crowd his house, bethought of engaging Master Betty, and offered him half the receipts after he had deducted the modest sum of twelve pounds for expenses. The boy was delighted at the proposition made him, and his parents consented to his appearance. He was therefore announced to play Osman, in the tragedy of *Zara*, on the 19th of August, 1803.

Curiosity drew a crowded audience, who expected to see a precocious boy trained to recite set speeches, and taught to assume a few stage attitudes. But their surprise was only equalled by their delight when they recognized in him a power capable of exciting their interests and swaying their feelings. A few nights after he played Douglas, and later on Rolla. The last character he attempted to represent at this theatre was Romeo. The fame of " little Betty," as he was generally called, spread far and near. Praise of his genius and predictions of his future were in all men's mouths; he was hailed as the wonder of his age. And his reputation reaching Dublin, Frederick Jones, manager of the

Crow Street Theatre, offered him an engagement for nine nights, which was readily accepted. It was accordingly advertised in the Dublin journals that "on Monday the 28th of November, 1803, the character of Douglas will be performed by a young gentleman only twelve years of age, whose admirable talents have procured him the deserved appellation of the Infant Roscius."

Age and youth, rank and fashion rushed to witness his performances and applaud his efforts. In the theatre he was greeted with enthusiasm; in private he was *fêted*. The nightly receipts of the playhouse amounted to four hundred pounds, an unusual sum. So successful was he, that the manager offered him an engagement for three years at an increasing salary, which the boy's father wisely refused. From Dublin he proceeded to Cork, where he received as salary a fourth part of the house, including a clear benefit; and from Cork he journeyed to Waterford, playing here in farce as well as in tragedy. Glasgow and Edinburgh were next visited by the Infant Roscius, who continued to draw crowded houses wherever and whenever he played. On his first appearance in the former city he was, says Jackson, the manager of the Edinburgh and Glasgow theatres, greeted "with the greatest bursts of applause I ever witnessed to have been given by an audience." He watched little Betty with a critic's eye, in order to notice his defects, and point them out if necessary; "but his correctness and graceful mode of deportment throughout the whole of the performance, and the astonishing exertions which his powers enabled him to exhibit, rendered useless my intention, and taught me to know that 'Nature's above art in that respect.' In the whole series of my acquaintance with the stage," he adds, "I have never beheld the same range of characters filled by the principal theatrical adults with a smaller number of admissible faults!"

In Edinburgh his reception was wildly enthusiastic. On the night he was announced to represent Douglas, Home, the author of the tragedy, came to the theatre, and sat at the first wing. Throughout the performance he showed strong signs of emotion,—the character which sprung from his imagination was visibly realized,—his words were hearkened to with breathless interest, his sentiments applauded by thousands, and when the curtain fell he was so carried away by his satisfaction and gratitude, that he rushed forward on the stage and bowed repeatedly, appropriating the enthusiasm to himself. His admiration for Master Betty knew no bounds;

embracing the lad, he declared him a " wonderful being, great beyond conception, one of the first actors on the British stage."

The Infant Roscius was now beset by offers of engagements on the most liberal terms from almost every manager of importance in Great Britain. He had already played in Ireland and Scotland, and, desirous of performing in England, decided on appearing at the Birmingham Theatre, of which Macready, father of the lad who afterwards became a notable actor, was then manager. His arrival here caused unusual sensation. Gentry from the surrounding districts poured into the town and crowded the hotels; his passage through the streets was attended by numbers who followed to catch sight of him; crowds thronged the doors of the theatre for hours before they were opened; portraits of him were exhibited in the windows of the print shops; and laudatory notices of him appeared in the press.

Now it happened that whilst he played at Birmingham, Mr. Justice Graham, one of the board of management which then ruled Drury Lane Theatre, passed through the town, and witnessing Master Betty's performance, was much struck by his talents. Reporting his impressions to the managers, they entered into negotiations with Betty senior, offering him half a clear benefit if his son would perform in their theatre for seven nights. This was indignantly rejected; and after some correspondence Macready's opinion was solicited regarding the salary young Roscius should receive. He declared the boy would be entitled to fifty guineas a night and a clear benefit; but these terms being considered excessive, the treaty was allowed to drop. Meanwhile Harris, manager of Covent Garden Theatre, entering into communication with Mr. Betty, engaged his son on the terms proposed. Hearing this, the managers of Drury Lane Theatre were wrathful, and immediately sent a trusty messenger to outbid their rival, and remind Mr. Betty they had made the first proposal. He replied Mr. Harris had made the first engagement, and he was in honour bound to him; however, as his agreement did not forbid young Roscius performing elsewhere in London on the intervening nights or weeks of his performances at Covent Garden, he was ready to enter into a compact with them by which the lad might appear at Drury Lane. His terms were now higher than those asked from Harris, the salary demanded being fifty pounds each for the first three nights' performances, and one hundred pounds for each succeeding night he played, with a clear benefit if the engagement was but for a fortnight, and two clear benefits if it lasted a month. The engagement was signed and sealed, binding him to appear in London in December; meanwhile he continued to play in the provinces.

The enthusiasm Master Betty created steadily increased. At Sheffield the prices of admission to the theatre were doubled, poems were addressed to him, people travelled from London to see him; and at Doncaster races scores of vehicles were labelled "Theatrical coaches to carry six insides to see the young Roscius." At Liverpool, where he acted fourteen nights, the rush to the box-office was so great in the morning, that men and women were bruised and crushed, hats and shoes were lost, and clothes were torn to pieces. For his services here he received fifteen hundred and twenty pounds, and the managers of the theatre offered him a like sum if he would play for an additional fourteen nights, but engagements already made prevented him accepting the offers. Before his departure they presented him with silver cups bearing inscriptions regarding their "profound respect for the most exalted talents of Master Betty." At Manchester, in consequence of the great confusion that had taken place, "whereby the lives of many people have been endangered," all application for tickets had to be made by letter; "all the letters," the manager advertised, "will be put into a bag, and, to secure the most perfect impartiality, two gentlemen will attend the drawing at eleven o'clock and see the places booked in the order they are drawn." Being prevented from playing during Passion week at Coventry, by the Bishop of Lichfield and Coventry, he stayed a day at Dunchurch. A lady, a member of one of the county families, who was on her way to Coventry to see the performance, was stopped at Dunchurch by news of his lordship's prohibition. Hearing that young Roscius was staying at the hotel where she rested, she immediately sent for the landlord, and begged of him to obtain her a sight of the lad, whom she would " give anything " to see. He assured her there was but one way by which her curiosity could be gratified, and that was by carrying in one of the dishes to table when Master Betty dined. The lady thanked him, and willingly agreed to wait upon the hero.

Rumours of his success and the sensation he caused reaching London, he was there anxiously awaited. Whilst at Leicester his father, who invariably accompanied him, received a letter from John Philip Kemble, then one of the proprietors and managers of Covent Garden Theatre, whose salary, it may be here remarked, of thirty-seven pounds sixteen shillings a week was less than Master Betty received for one night. "I cannot," he says, "hear of you being on your journey without doing myself the pleasure of expressing the satisfaction I feel in knowing that I shall soon have the happiness of welcoming you and Master Betty to Covent Garden Theatre ; and give me leave to say how heartily I congratulate the stage on the ornament and support it is, by the judgment of all the world, to receive from Master Betty's extraordinary talents and exertions. You will be much concerned to know that Mr. Harris has been for some time confined to his bed ; and, indeed, it has not been the least of his pains that his illness has prevented his gratifying himself, as he intended, by writing to you. If there is anything I can possibly do for you and Master Betty's accommodation against you come to town, pray command my best services."

His advent was now at hand, and London was in commotion. One evening, whilst Frederick Reynolds the dramatist was sitting in a box in the first circle of Covent Garden Theatre, a gentleman, accompanied by a very pretty boy, entered towards the beginning of the second act of the play, and sat beside him. The former asked which of the actors then on the stage was Kemble and which was Lewis, but the lad merely devoured oranges, and took no interest in the scene. Presently a fruit-woman entering, whispered to the dramatist that he was verily in the presence of Mr. Betty and his son; and on being asked how she knew, replied the superintendent of the free list, to whom they gave their names, had told her. She had scarcely communicated her news when the door was suddenly burst open, and hundreds of well-dressed persons, who had deserted their seats, sought to gain admission. News of Master Betty's presence in the house spread rapidly, and the crowd and excitement in and around the box became so great, that Mr. Betty in alarm called aloud for the box-keeper, but this individual not being able to approach because of the formidable numbers, Reynolds proposed to guide them into safety. As they with difficulty moved from the box, the crowd imagining they were about to leave the house, rushed to the lobby, where a better view of the prodigy might be had; on which Reynolds delivered young Roscius to the box-keeper, who quickly opened a private door leading to the green-room, where he and his father found refuge.

Saturday, the 1st of December, 1804, was fixed for his first appearance at Covent Garden Theatre. On the previous Friday night several persons had sought to conceal themselves in the house, in hope of being able to find a good position for witnessing his performance. About ten o'clock on the morning of the day he was announced to appear, men were seen to parade the piazza of the theatre, and collect in groups in various parts of Bow Street, that they might be near the doors when the crowd began to gather. All seats possible to book had been taken for the first six nights of Betty's performances. Soon after mid-day the principal entrances of the house were surrounded, and fresh batches continually arriving, quite early in the afternoon the piazza was not only full, but a mass of people compact and impenetrable stretched across the street. Danger was apprehended, and policemen were placed inside the building, whilst a detachment of the Guards was stationed outside. Before evening came the great heat and close pressure of the crowd became intolerable, and many persons fainted. The Guards now scattered those collected in the street, and stationing themselves at the entrance to the piazza, allowed none to add to the numbers already collected there.

The doors were opened at half-past four o'clock, when a terrific rush like that of a released torrent poured into the house. Indescribable confusion followed. Before five minutes had elapsed the galleries were crowded to their uttermost limit. The pit was crammed, and many of those who held pit tickets climbed into the front boxes, and refused to move from their position; the passages and lobbies were likewise filled by those who, unable to obtain places, were satisfied to remain in the building, though they could neither see nor hear young Roscius. The din resounding through the house was deafening; cries and remonstrances, laughter and gossip filled the air. Presently the heat became unendurable, and long before the play began, and continually during the performance, men and women fainted. The Prince of Wales, afterwards George the Fourth, fat and florid in a tight coat, red-brown wig, and many-folded neckcloth, sat in Lady Melbourne's box; crowds of fair women and notable men gathered in the surrounding circle, a blaze of diamonds and decorations in all; whilst behind the scenes, actors, dramatists, and critics assembled in numbers, satisfied to witness the performance from the wings. After patient waiting and strong endurance, the audience saw the curtain rise. Then the play, *Barbarossa*, began, but Achmet, the character Master Betty represented, not appearing in the first act, no heed was paid to the players, whose voices were drowned in the continued murmuring and general excitement.

At the beginning of the second act silence settled over the house, and when at last the boy made his appearance whom they had suffered so much to see, thunders of applause echoed and re-echoed through the theatre. With admirable self-possession and apparent calmness he bowed repeatedly, undismayed by the vast mass of faces rising tier above tier before him. Then turning to the stage he began his part, seeming to lose all knowledge of his audience in the identity of his representation. . In appearance he was slight and feminine, his features clear cut and intelligent in expression, his eyes small, his bright brown hair falling, after the fashion of the day, in ringlets on his shoulders. His voice was rather monotonous, and in the higher notes decidedly shrill. He was continually interrupted by the plaudits of his audience, and when the act concluded deafening cheers rang through the house. Throughout the tragedy the enthusiasm increased, and at its conclusion the audience, by way of compliment to Master Betty, refused to permit the usual farce to be played.

Having acted six nights at Covent Garden, he began his performances at Drury Lane. Here the scene which had taken place at the rival house on his first appearance was repeated with additional violence;

for the crowd outside the theatre, impatient of the long delay which ensued before the doors were opened, smashed all the windows within reach; whilst on gaining admission it destroyed the balustrades leading to the boxes and galleries, and forced the bars at the pay-doors.

Honours now poured thick upon Master Betty. By their request he was presented to George III. and Queen Charlotte; the Prince of Wales entertained him at Carlton House; he was proposed as a fitting subject for the Cambridge prize medal poem; invitations from the highest women in the land were showered upon him; ducal carriages were placed at his disposal, and carried him to and from the theatres; Opie painted him as Norval on the Grampian hills; Northcote represented him in full length with Shakespeare standing at a respectful distance; busts of him were exhibited at the exhibitions; whilst prints displayed in the shop-windows portrayed John Philip Kemble and himself riding on one horse, Master Betty in front, remarking, "I don't mean to affront you, but when two persons ride on a horse one must be behind."

But what was perhaps the most flattering compliment of all awaited him. One night, when he was playing Achmet at Drury Lane, it was whispered that

Gentleman Smith, the original Charles Surface, who had retired some sixteen years previously, was now in the house. And the tragedy being ended, this excellent actor went behind the scenes, and requested he might be introduced to the boy. This being accomplished, they fell into discourse, when Gentleman Smith said, "During Garrick's last illness he gave me a seal, his own likeness cut whilst in Italy, with this commission, that should I in after years meet with a player who acted from nature and from feeling, and whom I considered worthy of the gift, I should present him with that token. I have travelled from Bury St. Edmunds to be present at your performance, and I consider you worthy of the valued relic." A few days later the seal reached Master Betty with the following letter—

"YOUNG GENTLEMAN,

"The fame of your talents has drawn an old fellow-labourer in the theatric vineyard from his retirement in a very advanced age, and he feels well rewarded for his trouble. Let me recommend to you strict attention to the arts and *belles lettres*. May your success continue, and may you live to be an ornament to the stage and to your country. Accept from me the seal of our great predecessor—a strong likeness of Mr. Garrick.

> " Couldst thou in this engravèd pebble trace
> The living likeness of his plastic face,
> Whilst thy congenial soul partook its fire,
> His magic eye thy spirit would inspire.

"I am your admirer, friend, and well-wisher,

"W. SMITH."

"*Feb.* 15, 1805."

His London engagements brought great profit to himself and to the theatres at which he played. The receipts of Drury Lane for the twenty-eight nights during which he performed amounted to seventeen thousand two hundred and ten pounds, being an average sum of six hundred and fourteen pounds nightly; his own salary for these evenings being two thousand seven hundred and eighty-two pounds, independent of his benefits, which realized about two thousand guineas. Having gained unexpected wealth and renown in London, he returned to the provinces, but in the following winter he was again announced to appear at both theatres during the months of December, 1805, and January, 1806. Meanwhile curiosity concerning him had considerably abated, and though the House of Commons on one occasion, at the desire of his friend Mr. Pitt, adjourned to witness his performance of *Hamlet*, yet his audiences were by no means so large as during his first visit. Indeed, the receipts taken on the evenings he played at Drury Lane Theatre were little more than half the sums received the previous year, and averaged but two hundred and twenty-seven pounds some odd shillings nightly. A month before his second visit a lady of the mature age of eight years, whose acting had created a sensation in the provinces, was, whilst playing Miss Peggy in the *Country Girl* at Drury Lane Theatre, hissed off the stage, and not permitted to finish her part, though she made a pert speech in her own defence. This was a sign to Master Betty, whose career as a phenomenon was almost at an end.

Actors deserving well of the town, whose positions had been hardly won, were from the first indignant at the foolish enthusiasm that the immature acting of a clever boy had caused. Mrs. Siddons and John Kemble had withheld from appearing in the same cast with Betty, and it was with reluctance the members of the company at either house performed with him. Above all others Kean, who possessed a full sense of his own worth, was wrath that this lad's mechanical performances should produce wealth and fame, whilst he, who was gifted with fire, imagination, passion, and capacity, almost starved; and this feeling within him presently resolved itself into action. Meantime Master Betty, whom we shall meet again, returned once more to the provinces, where he continued to reap golden harvests.

It was the custom for Drury Lane and Covent Garden Theatres to close from the end of June to early in September, during which time a summer season of performances was held at the Haymarket Theatre, the players chiefly consisting of minor lights from the great houses, with an occasional star from some provincial theatre introduced by way of novelty and attraction. The luminary whom it was hoped would shine this season was Alexander Rae, who had formerly played Richmond to Kean's Richard in the back parlour of Mrs. Price's house. He was five years older than the friend of his boyhood, and had begun life as clerk to an army agent, but having a passion for the stage, he became an actor. His presence was handsome and attractive, his playing brisk and noisy. In tragedy and comedy he showed an equal talent, which never rose above the dull level of mediocrity. Mrs. Siddons, who had acted with him in Liverpool, had said that, "out of London there was nothing to equal this young fellow;" and though her judgment was found wanting, yet when spoken by her it was heard as the utterance of an oracle, and he had been engaged forthwith for the Haymarket.

On this opening night of the season, June 9th, 1806, Rae played Octavian, a favourite character of Kean's, who had acted it in the provinces with great success. But no chance was afforded him of appearing in a prominent part, though, according to one who knew him well, he was now "a better actor than he could have been in 1830, when sickness had enervated his frame, and when his defects had become habits by the flattery of ill-judging friends and the applause of name-lauding auditors." But those surrounding him were blind to his merits, and had he laid bare his pretentions they would have laughed him to scorn. To them this slight-figured, shabbily-dressed youth, with eager dark eyes and reticent manners, was but a member of impoverished strolling companies, who had fared over-well in receiving an engagement in London. Though the parts he played were insignificant, the manner in which he acted them was excellent, but his fellow-labourers were the last to admit his ability. When in a drama of Colman's, called *Means and Ways*, he acted the part of Carney, a slight outline which he developed into a character, those watching him at the wings whispered to each other, "He's trying to act; the little fellow's making a part of Carney;" to which remark came the reply, "He wants fun, and is too real."

The public were more kind, and occasional approbation rewarded his endeavours. He was proud to recall that once he received three rounds of applause for delivering a few words; and again, when *Five Miles Off, or the Finger Post*, was produced, its author, Thomas Dibdin, publicly commended his acting of a very trivial part. His feelings of mortification at the estimate in which he was held behind the curtain, and at the opportunities denied him of appearing in prominent parts, were heightened by Rae's forgetfulness of their boyish friendship; one was seemingly at the head of his profession, playing lead in a London house, the other was at the lowest rung of the ladder, and the distance lying between was great. One day whilst rehearsing the *Iron Chest*, in which Rae was cast for Sir Edward Mortimer and Kean for a nameless servant, the former, in changing the business of the last act, gave some directions to the latter which he did not immediately understand, and the passage was therefore repeated three times, when at last Rae exclaimed, "Never mind, sir, we'll try it at night." One who was present says he believes Rae unintentionally spoke the words in that hopeless tone men use when despairing of making others understand their meaning. "Kean's brow changed," says this observer, "a look which I have since marked often came over his pale face, and a peculiar motion of his lips as if he were chewing or swallowing, which in Kean was a certain sign of hurt feeling or supposed rage. I do not believe that Kean ever forgot that circumstance."

To drown his sense of disappointment he too often frequented the Antelope tavern, then kept by one Clarke, who had been kind to him in Sheerness during days of weariness and weeks of hardship. Shy, silent, and perhaps scornful, he avoided Finche's, to which the better class of players resorted to recount their late success or predict their future triumphs—language which, to one holding within him the elements of greatness fate denied him the opportunity of testing, might well goad him to madness. The season at the Haymarket ended on the 12th of September. Before that date Kean, carrying with him a letter of introduction to John Philip Kemble, waited on him at Covent Garden Theatre that he might request an engagement. Kemble's manner, perhaps charged with the remembrance of his mimicry in the past, was cold and

severe ; Kean left his presence chilled and depressed,
and stated he would rather never play in London than
act under Kemble. Soon he received an engagement,
at a salary of eighteen shillings a week, from Mrs. Baker,
a manageress well-known in the provinces, and played
at Tunbridge Wells on the 22nd of the month. It
is worthy of note, that Kean, Mrs. Siddons, and George
Frederick Cooke had failed to attract attention on
their first appearances in London. Each had then gone
back to the country, where Mrs. Siddons remained seven
years, Cooke two-and-twenty, and Kean eight years,
before returning to the capital and securing success.

Mr. Kean " of the Theatre Royal, Haymarket," as he
was now styled in the playbills, frequently figured as
first tragedian, occasionally as light comedian, and
generally as a singer of comic songs between the acts.
He then began a career heavily chequered by success
and failure, by light and shadow, which eventually
ended in renown. Determined to gain fame, he continually studied, and whilst at Birmingham resolved on
representing Hamlet. Parts of the play he had recited
in days of yore to Miss Tidswell, or enacted for the
benefit of Mrs. Clarke's guests, but he now for the first
time represented the grief-stricken prince as a complete
figure in the tragic picture Shakespeare has painted for

all time. His study was slow and careful, and those who were stirred by his outbursts seldom considered the labour they cost him; what they deemed the result of inspiration had been carefully rehearsed; for even genius must labour to excel. Mrs. Kean was wont in after years to narrate that he " used to mope about for hours, walking miles and miles alone with his hands in his pockets, thinking intensely on his characters. No one," she added, "could get a word from him. He studied and slaved beyond any actor I ever knew."

His appearance as Hamlet received the success it merited, and was repeated several times during the company's stay in that town; he had now made a step forward towards the goal he desired. Soon after, he travelled into Scotland, and from there passed over to Belfast, where Atkins engaged him to play leading parts. Arriving here, he was told that two nights later Mrs. Siddons would give a few performances at the theatre, beginning with the *Mourning Bride*, in which he was cast for Osmyn, a part with which he was wholly un-familiar. He immediately assured Atkins it would be impossible for him to attempt the character, but the manager answered he had engaged himself to play principal parts, and must fulfil his contract. The young actor confessed his memory was slow to grasp or retain, and that it would be an act of injustice to himself, and likewise to Mrs. Siddons, to force this representation upon him; but Atkins would hear of no refusal.

Accordingly he prepared to face the situation. He had previously accepted an invitation from a friend on board a sloop of war lying in Carrickfergus Bay to dine with him on Sunday. On Friday evening he betook himself to this friend, that he might study in greater peace and seclusion, and returned on Monday, believing his efforts had been successful. A densely-packed audience awaited the great actress, who was received with enthusiasm; then silence fell upon the house. Kean began his part, spoke the first few lines, hesitated, and paused; the impressive bearing of Mrs. Siddons, the breathless attention of the crowd made him forget his lines. Approaching the wings, he sought to catch the prompter's words, but in striving to repeat them spoke nonsense, and ended in failure. Nothing but the presence of Mrs. Siddons suppressed the gradually increasing anger of the assemblage, and to appease its fury he came forward and explained the circumstances under which he was obliged to act.

Venice Preserved was the next play in which Mrs. Siddons was to appear, a rehearsal for which was called next morning. Before it began, she asked who was to represent Jaffier? Kean's name was mentioned. "What!" said she, indignantly, "surely not that horrid little man who destroyed the tragedy last night!" The manager assured her he was perfect in his part, and would play it extremely well. His judgment proved correct; for not only did Kean please the audience, but likewise the queen of tragedy, who complimented him on his performance, and foretold his success. The words of encouragement he had previously received had been few, and those of so famous a woman were welcome as gifts; they served as oil to light the flame of hope.

At the conclusion of his engagement at Belfast he joined Watson's company, which made periodical circuits of the chief towns of Gloucester, Warwick, Worcester, and Hertfordshire, playing tragedy, ccmedy, farce, and pantomime. One evening whilst he was acting at Birmingham in a pantomime, founded on the story of Alonzo the Brave and the Fair Imogene, a school-boy aged sixteen named William Charles Macready, then home from Rugby for the holidays, sat in a box with his sister to witness the performance. The principal characters were represented by Richer, a baron all covered with jewels and gold; by Mrs. Watson, a female porpoise, ungainly and gaudy, who played the beauteous

Imogene; and Kean, clad in green satin as became
Alonzo the Brave. "It was so ridiculous," says Macready, "that the only impression I carried away was
that the hero and heroine were the worst in the piece.
How little did I know, or could guess, that under that
shabby green satin dress was hidden one of the most
extraordinary theatrical geniuses that have ever illus-
trated the dramatic poetry of England.   When some
years afterwards public enthusiasm was excited to the
highest pitch by the appearance at Drury Lane of an
actor of the name of Kean, my astonishment may easily
be concerned in discovering that the little insignificant
Alonzo the Brave was the grandly impassioned personater
of Othello, Richard, and Shylock."

CHAPTER III.

AND now was an important event in his life's history
at hand. Whilst at Cheltenham an Irish girl named
Mary Chambers joined the company. She was a native
of Waterford, and in the capacity of governess had
travelled with a family named Congreve, of Mount
Congreve, county Waterford, to Cheltenham, where
they repaired to drink the waters. Weary of the
drudgery of a school-room, and believing she possessed
dramatic talent, she determined to become an actress,
and selected Cheltenham as the scene of her *début*.

She danced gracefully, sang prettily, but acted indifferently. Her manners were kindly and gentle, her voice soft and sweet, and her appearance refined if not handsome. From the tasteful manner in which she invariably dressed, as well as from her general appearance, Kean, without any false representation of hers, came to believe she possessed some money, and, anxious to better his condition, proposed marriage to her, he being at this time in his twenty-first year, while she was nine years older.

He was immediately accepted, and one bright morning, on the 17th of July, 1808, this marriage, loveless at least on his side, was celebrated in the parish church of Stroud, in the county of Gloucester, by the Rev. Mr. Adams, whose fee Kean paid out of half-a-sovereign lent him by Miss Harriet Thornton, who figured on this occasion as a bridesmaid. Returning to Cheltenham, the wedding party hastened to the Dog Tavern, where its worthy hostess, Mrs. Hyell, furnished the poor players with a wedding breakfast at her own expense. Kean's salary at the time when he became a husband was a guinea a week. Some months after his marriage he left Watson's company to join the troop of another manager named Cherry, who gave him twenty-five shillings a week.

Andrew Cherry was a clever dramatist, an excellent comedian, and an able manager. Moreover was he a man of wit. It is recorded of him, that before taking a company into the country he was offered a remunerative engagement by the proprietor of a theatre who on a former occasion had cheated him. Therefore his brief answer was, that he " had bit him once, and was now resolved he would not have two bites of A. Cherry." When Kean and his wife joined him he was travelling with a fairly good company through South Wales and the south-west of Ireland. Kean's engagement had been made by letter, and there now arose a difficulty regarding his joining Cherry at Swansea. Neither he nor his wife, soon to become a mother, had money to defray their travelling expenses, and it but remained for them to make the journey on foot. Accordingly these poor strollers, ill-clad, badly fed, and lacking strength, trudged wearily along the high roads for many days, now reciting and singing with what spirits they could summon at some village inn, that they might secure a night's shelter; again playing in a barn, that they might earn a meal from the pittance wrung from over-fed, gaping, witless rustics. Their fatigue and hardships were great, and their exhaustion complete, when they reached their destination, and received some funds in advance from the manager to supply their wants.

When Kean was sufficiently recovered to join the company, he was somewhat disappointed at finding the principal parts were generally allotted to a tragedian named Smith ; but his spirits rose on seeing this actor's deficiency, for he chiefly depended for his effects on rant, and tore his passions to tatters. Strength of lung in shouting, and force of limb in gesticulating, stood in place of facial expression or intellectual interpretation. Kean endured him with such patience as kindly heaven granted him, until one night, when Smith was playing Hamlet, and Kean representing the venerable Polonius. Then did his endurance gradually vanish, until at the conclusion of the play scene, where the king calls for lights, Kean, overcome by the ridiculous bearing of Hamlet, and the idiotic behaviour of the whole court of Denmark, suddenly threw a double somersault, which by its daring novelty electrified not only the noble company upon the stage, but the admiring audience likewise.

An explanation with the manager followed this unrehearsed action, the result being, that Kean was allowed to play the heroes of tragedy henceforth. Now the sometime Hamlet accepted his fate with philosophy, but felt inclined to take his revenge when opportunity offered. This came to him in due course. One night when Kean played Richard III., and the tragedy had arrived at the scene where the body of Henry VI. is being carried past Richard, one of the supers, who, to make the scene more realistic, was dressed as a parson, coughed violently, whereon Smith, once a Danish prince, but now a corpse-bearer, instead of saying, "My lord, stand back, and let the coffin pass," cried out in impressive accents, "My lord, stand back, and let the parson cough," which so tickled the fancy of Henry's disconsolate widow, that she burst into loud laughter, and the whole scene was spoilt. Kean now played a round of characters in which he subsequently won fame, and was regarded by many as a player whose future promised fair success.

Whilst at Swansea Mrs. Kean gave birth to their first child, named Howard, to whom Kean became passionately devoted. From this town the company travelled to Carmarthen and Haverfordwest, playing a season in each place, and then crossed the Channel to Waterford. Whilst in this city the troop was joined by an Irishman named Sheridan Knowles, who, like many another ambitious youth, without possessing ability as an actor, believed himself destined for the stage. Having given up his appointment in a London hospital, he had made his *début* as Hamlet before a Dublin audience; but such talent as he betrayed was insufficient to impress his manager with ardent desires to secure his services. Therefore he had gone into the provinces as a strolling player, married Maria Charteris, and eventually joined Cherry's company at Waterford. With Kean this round-faced, genial-tempered, bustling little man soon became fast friends; and his admiration for the young tragedian begot the desire to write him a play. Accordingly, Sheridan Knowles laboured and brought forth his first drama, entitled *Leo, or the Gipsy*, in which Kean played the hero with credit to himself and profit to the author, for whose benefit it was produced.

It was not merely the principal characters in tragedy and comedy Kean was engaged to perform; occasionally he was expected to use his energies as a ballet-master, and show his agility as a harlequin; and on more than one occasion he acted the latter on the same evening that he played Richard III. But, notwithstanding his excellent performances, and the various attractions held forth by the theatre, audiences were scant in number; and Kean was wont to relate that scarce ever had he felt hunger so acutely as one night, when playing *King Lear* to the dull and honest burghers of this goodly city; the pangs of his empty stomach gave a wildness to his eye which no effort of imagination could produce.

It happened during the course of Cherry's stay in this city, a young subaltern named Grattan, and his friend a little lieutenant of artillery, were stationed at the barracks. Now as both these youths were strolling one summer evening along the Mall, where the theatre was situated, they paused to read a glaring play-bill, announcing the tragedy of *Hamlet* would be acted by the full strength of the company on that date. Kean was set down to represent the Prince, Cherry for Polonius, and Sheridan Knowles for Rosencrantz, a fact which held out no attraction for them. However, as they prided themselves on their skill in using the foils, they mutually expressed a desire to witness the fencing scene between Hamlet and Laertes. To their mental capacities the first four acts of the great tragedy was considered a trial beyond endurance, but they resolved to see the fifth, and judge "what sort of affair the strollers would make of it."

Having signified their gracious intentions to the door-keeper that he might call them when the time arrived, they meanwhile betook themselves to a neighbouring billiard-room in pursuit of an amusement that might not overtax their intellects. In the course of the evening the door-keeper came to announce that the fifth act was about to begin, and with a correct absence of excitement, they leisurely strolled towards the play-house, and took possession of a stage box. They were in time to hear Osric's invitation to Hamlet "lisped out with the usual vulgar caricature of court foppery regularly exhibited by theatre royal comedians, as well as by our Waterford candle-snuffer," writes the magnificent Grattan. When the fencing began poor Osric's desperate efforts had merely the effect of amusing them, and they turned their kind attention to the chief actors in the scene. He who played Laertes being tall of stature made Hamlet's representation appear more diminutive than he really was. The fight between them began, when so poor was their skill in the eyes of the lieutenant, himself a practised swordsman, as he would have the world know, that he laughed aloud in his scorn, and crying out theatrically "Hold, enough," requested his companion to leave the house. Grattan would have gone with him, had he not noticed the extreme skill and grace with which Kean parried the cut-and-thrust attacks of his adversary, and saw, moreover, the look of haughty resentment he turned upon the swaggering lieutenant on hearing him laugh. As the duel continued, Grattan's admiration of Kean's carriage and action increased, and when the curtain fell his curiosity concerning him was roused.

Therefore in passing out he made inquiries regarding Kean from the money-taker, a garrulous dame, well versed in the private histories of the company individually and collectively. From her he learned that Kean was an actor of talent, the first tragedian of the company, likewise its principal singer, stage manager, inventor of pantomimes and ballets of action, and the best harlequin in Ireland, Wales, or the West of England. Moreover, it was added he gave lessons in fencing and boxing, for his skill with both foils and gloves was known to many. Hearing these things the young men sought his acquaintance, and engaged that he should give them lessons in fencing, though, adds Grattan, "his visits were not made in the capacity of master, for we were either of us quite a match for him." Whilst giving instructions in the rooms of his pupils, he made acquaintance with the officers of the garrison, all of whom admired his dexterity in fencing; and they, falling at odd times into conversation with him, and witnessing his various talents, became interested in his fortunes, and resolved on securing him a well-filled house on the night of his benefit.

The play Kean selected for this occasion was Hannah More's tragedy of *Percy*, in which he represented the hero and Mrs. Kean the heroine. Whilst the company stayed at Waterford her name had not appeared on the play-bills, for before arriving in her native city Kean had requested the manager to waive her engagement; for, insomuch as the heroines were represented by other ladies of the company, she could only appear in inferior characters, a fact that might prejudice her in the opinion of her connections and friends. This sacrifice of her salary for the benefit of his pride was made at a time when he could ill-afford the loss of even such a trifling sum. Mrs. Kean's appearance on the occasion of her husband's benefit was described in the bills as "her first upon any stage;" probably a precaution taken to insure the needed mercy of her audience. The house was crowded by those whom either curiosity or friendship drew to witness her efforts, as well as by the military element attracted by Kean.

On this night he displayed various talents, in all of which he excelled; for having roused the sympathies of his audience by his tragic power, he gave a specimen of his skill as a tight-rope dancer, an art he had learned in Saunders' circus, then sparred with a professional pugilist, took the leading part in a musical interlude, and finally performed Chimpanzee the monkey in the melodramatic pantomime of *La Perouse*, and in the death scene exhibited a pathos and feeling that made his audience weep. This benefit brought him the welcome sum of forty pounds. His visit to Waterford was made memorable not only by this unusual windfall of fortune, but likewise because of the birth of his second son Charles.

From Waterford the company proceeded to Clonmel, where Kean's excellent acting created attention, and where likewise he was, as in Waterford, enabled to add to his income by teaching fencing. And having tarried some months in this town they crossed over to Swansea, where the youngest sister of the great Mrs. Siddons, Mrs. Hutton, then lived. This offspring of a clever family had no dramatic talent, but was well-known as the author of several tales written under the *nom de plume* of Anne of Swansea. She was struck by Kean's various powers, and to better his fortune, and perhaps gratify her vanity, wrote a play for him, in which he performed for his benefit.

He had now been over two years in Cherry's

company, and had steadily gained in reputation; and
knowing he had benefited his manager, he asked an
increase of ·five shillings a week in his salary; but this
Cherry refused, and they parted.   Once more Kean
had the world before him.   Hearing a vacancy had
occurred in the Bath Theatre, he offered his services,
but preference was given to another applicant; he
then wrote to the manager of a Liverpool theatre, who
replied that his company was full.   Once more taking
heart, he communicated with Frederick Jones of the
Crow Street Theatre, Dublin, stating he would act
tragedy and comedy, and serve as master of the ballet,
for three pounds a week, but his proposal was declined.
He then travelled to town, hoping to find an engagement there, no matter how humble, which might save
him from the drudgery of a strolling player's life.
Penniless as he was, he and his family endured much.
"At Richmond in Yorkshire," Mrs. Kean wrote, " we
suffered more than common privations.   My husband
took a room in the principal inns, and gave recitations,
singing, &c.   A gentleman who kept a large establishment for the education of young gentlemen was very
kind, and the young gentlemen called next day with
their pocket-money, and left it with the landlady
directed for Mr. Kean, the sum amounting, I think,

to eleven shillings and sixpence. There is something in the generosity of youth." Arriving footsore and weary in town, disappointment awaited him, but still he struggled. At length he heard that Hughes, then manager of the Weymouth, Plymouth, and Exeter theatres, was in want of a clever actor, and applying to him, Kean was engaged to play tragedy and comedy, farce and pantomime, at a salary of two guineas a week. But now having spent his money by his journey to town and his residence there, he knew not how he might reach Weymouth, until at last coming to hear that his new manager's father held an engagement at Sadlers Wells Theatre, he addressed him the following letter, in which he refers with some exaggeration to his large family and most expensive baggage, and shows a certain amount of affectation in the use of Latin and Greek.

"Tavistock Row, Covent Garden, 1812.

"*To* — HUGHES, ESQ., *Sadlers Wells Theatre.*

"DEAR SIR,

"Having travelled lately some hundred Miles with a large family and most expensive baggage, I am left in London in a situation (which many of our brother professionals are acquainted with) *Non est mihi*

argentum. It is My wish therefore to depart by to-
morrow's coach for Weymouth, but I frankly confess
I at present have not the means; if, sir, you would
oblige me with the sum of ten pounds, Mr. Finch or
Miss Tidswell will become Answerable for my immediate appearance at Weymouth, and Mr. Hughes might
proceed to the reduction of ten shillings per week till
the debt is discharged. As I am fully sensible this is
a great obligation from a stranger, it is my wish to pay
any interest on the money you may please to demand,
and as Mr. Hughes, Junr. will have the means in his
own hands, there can be no *doubt* of the payment, and
I shall bear the recollection of your kindness παρ ὅλον
τὸν βίον. I should not ask so great a favour, but My
Aunt, whose purse was ever open to my necessities, is at
this moment as bare in pocket as Myself, and another
Relation from whom I have been in the habit of receiving Supplies is not in London. I can only say, sir,
however exorbitant the request may appear to a
stranger, there is no Manager who *knows me* would
refuse it; it is My intention, should fortune favour my
designs, to make the Situation you have offered me a
permanency, and as I have ever shown unremitting
attention to my professional duties, I despair not of
joining your approbation to the public's, and of making

it pleasant to all parties. The money I write for is for immediate service, and if you would commit it to the charge of the bearer—My Servant—it would be brought very safe to Me, and to-morrow we would depart for Weymouth.

> "I am, Sir,
>
> "With the greatest Respect, Yours,
>
> "E. KEAN.

"P.S.—If it is your wish to see me on the business, and you will appoint the hour, I'll wait upon you, but I shall be greatly distressed if I cannot procure the money to-day."

A sum sufficient for his travelling expenses was lent him, and he joined the company at Weymouth, from whence it moved to Exeter. Here he and his family occupied rooms in Goldsmith Street, situated behind All Hallows Church. The audiences of this quiet cathedral town prided themselves on their critical judgment. They knew a good play when they saw it, and had beheld great tragedians in their day, so that when they pronounced Kean to be fairly excellent, he was certainly gratified. To them he played Hamlet, Richard III., Othello, and Shylock, representing the latter as an injured and pathetic figure instead of presenting him as an object for the scoffs and scorn of the gallery, as most actors did at this time. This change caused considerable debate amongst the lovers of Shakspeare; essays and pamphlets were written on the subject, and debates held concerning the great dramatist's idea of the Jew.

Kean had the good fortune whilst here to attract the notice and gain the friendship of a worthy resident, one Mr. Nation, an old gentleman famous for his knowledge of Shakspeare and his love of the stage. Appreciating Kean's genius, he had become interested in his fate, and striven to forward his fortunes. Inviting him to his house, he entertained him, read plays with him, and debated regarding the meaning of various passages and the delivery of certain parts. To these conversations the young tragedian attributed many of the excellences which subsequently marked his representations. Nor did the offices of friendship end here. In order to draw the attention of London managers to Kean's performances, this ingenious man would write criticisms on them, dwell on their various merits, refer to the crowded audiences who witnessed them, and the applause that greeted them, both these latter details being purely imaginary. These critiques he handed to one Marjerum, a correspondent for the metropolitan papers, who forwarded them to town ; and they appearing in due time, the good people of Exeter wondered · exceedingly at the false rumours spread abroad concerning themselves and their theatre, whilst Kean and his patron enjoyed them as capital jokes.

But Mr. Nation's efforts on Kean's behalf did not end here. Being personally acquainted with Dr. Drury, head-master of Harrow, and knowing him to be a lover of good acting, and moreover a man of influence, he begged him to come and stay a night at Exeter, that he might witness Kean's playing. With this request the doctor complied, and accompanying his friend to the theatre, was so forcibly struck by Kean's representation of Cato, that he promised to use what interest he had with the managers of Drury Lane in urging them to give this actor a trial; and as he promised so did he perform, but no immediate result followed his exertions on the actor's behalf.

Whilst Kean was playing at Exeter, William Henry Betty, now arrived at the age of manhood, came to the theatre as a star. He had retired from the stage for upwards of six years, four of which he had spent as a student at Cambridge ; but anxious to trade upon his former reputation and accumulate more wealth, he once more trod the boards. He is described at this period as being " a great lubberly, overgrown, fat-voiced, good-tempered fellow, with very little talent, and just tolerated as a man by those who were ashamed to confess they were deceived in thinking him a divinity when a boy." His figure indeed was much too large and heavy for the stage, his actions overstrained, exuberant, unnatural, and though not wholly destitute of grace, yet generally laboured. His tread on the boards " more resembled the awkward stride of a caricature performer in pantomime than the graceful walk of a tragic hero, whilst his voice was coarse and provincial."

His fame had not wholly died during his retirement, and his name was yet sufficient to ensure full houses whenever he performed. Now Kean, hearing he was coming to Exeter, became exceedingly uneasy, and when Betty arrived his wrath overflowed; for the appreciation and reward denied to merit were freely given to one who lived on his reputation as a clever boy; and when presently asked to play Laertes to Betty's Hamlet, he flatly refused. A writer who contributed some memoranda to the *Literary Gazette* says, that on returning from the theatre one night in a drizzling rain he encountered Kean. " He had been wandering about the whole night, unable to endure the mortification he experienced. I reasoned with him," continues this individual, "but it was in vain. 'I must feel deeply,' he replied; 'he commands overflowing houses, I play to empty benches, and I know my powers are superior to his.'"

His belief in his own talents, notwithstanding the slights he received and the appreciation he lacked, was firm; and frequently he predicted his future greatness, for he was still young, and hope dwells with youth.

Probably his manager shared Kean's opinion of himself, for he was not dismissed because of his refusal to support Mr. Betty, and on the departure of that actor continued to play leading parts. His marriage had not made him a man of more sober habits, and occasionally he and his family felt the misery of want. Not that he was ever unwilling to spare his labours; that he might add to his salary, he taught elocution, dancing, and fencing, but he spent his money as freely as he had earned it hardly. The straits to which his extravagance reduced him were sometimes cruel. One day the barber who was nightly engaged at the theatre, and every morning assisted Mr. Nation in his toilet, a verbose, kindly gossip, made complaint to the latter. "Is it not a scandal, sir," quoth Figaro, sadly, "that such a man as Mr. Kean should be so badly treated? Yesterday evening he wanted a pint of porter to enable him to continue his part, and he hadn't twopence, nor would the publican give him credit; but I," continued the barber proudly, "I lent him the money."

Desiring greatly to gain a footing in one of the London theatres, he wrote from time to time offering his services to their managers, giving references to Andrew Cherry, Anne of Swansea, and Dr. Drury, but in most cases no answer was vouchsafed to the poor stroller. Still with eager eyes he looked down the road of time to sight his coming fame, and saw behind every cloud the herald of good tidings. One day, when it was told him Lord and Lady Cork had bespoken *Othello* for that evening, he thought his fortune was now surely made, for his lordship, who had gained some reputation for judgment as a theatrical critic, must necessarily be impressed with his merits, and would no doubt use his influence towards directing the world's attention to his playing. Accordingly he exerted his abilities to their utmost, but neither the sweetness of his voice nor the force of his acting had power to win the attention of his lordship, who amused himself by watching his children playing at hot cockles in front of the box, whilst Kean spoke the finest speeches of Othello. That night his spirits were heavily depressed; his evil planet was still in the ascendant.

At the suggestion of one of his friends, he studied the part of Zanga for his benefit. But the wardrobe of the theatre not being rich in its resources, and containing for the most part doublets of rusty velvet and suits of faded satin adorned with tarnished tinsel, Kean was at a loss how to dress a character whose sole costume should properly consist of a tiger or leopard skin. But necessity urging invention, he secured from a mahogany table a brass claw, to which he fastened a calemanco robe, and thus adorned he appeared before a wondering audience. His performance in the tragedy was noble and impressive, but many of those who filled the theatre that evening preferred him as harlequin in the pantomime of *The Judgment of Paris* which followed. As a harlequin he frequently appeared, yet he could not endure the character, which the commands of his manager alone compelled him to play. "I never feel degraded," he was wont to say, "but when I have the motley jacket on my back."

For all that the motley jacket was continually on his back, and there were many amongst the Exeter audiences who thought his harlequinade superior to his tragedy. On the close of the winter season 1813, he placed his benefit under the patronage of Mrs. Buller of Downes, selecting *Cato* as the play for the evening.

The play-bill, a copy of which is given here, is still extant.

MR. KEAN'S NIGHT.

Under the Immediate Patronage of Mrs. Buller of Downes.

On Friday Evening, March 26th, 1813,

Will be presented (not acted here these 20 years)
Addison's celebrated PLAY of

CATO.

" Cuncta terrarum subæta
Præter atrocem animum Catonis."

M. P. Cato (the Roman Quæstor) ... ... MR. KEAN
Portius ... MR. HAMILTON. Marcus ... MR. TOKELEY
Sempronius } Roman Senators ... ... { MR. PERKINS
Lucius } { MR. WORSDALE
Syphax (the Numidian General) ... ... MR. MASON
Decius (Ambassador from Cæsar) ... ... MR. CONGDON
Juba (the Prince of Zama) ... ... MR. LOVEDAY
Marcia ... MISS RIVERS. Lucia ... MISS QUANTRELL

After which, by particular desire, the Popular Burlesque Tragic
OPERA called

BOMBASTES FURIOSO.

As performed upwards of 100 nights at the Theatre Royal,
Haymarket.

Artaxominous (King of Utopia) ... ... MR. TOKELEY
Fusbos (Minister of State) ... ... MR. PERKINS
First Courtier...MR. ESWOOD. Second Courtier...MR. CONGDON
General Bombastus ... ... MR. BENNETT
Distassma ... ... MRS. M. HUGHES

To conclude with an Entire New PANTOMIME (with original music, &c.), called

THE SAVAGES.

Got up under the immediate direction of MR. KEAN.

Korah (Husband to Illa)	MR. KEAN
Kojah (Confederate of Yassedo) ..., ...	MR. CONGDON
Powtanowski ... MR. WORSDALE. Zenoni ...	MR. ESWOOD
Swampum	MR. GREGORY
Yaffedo (secretly in Love with Illa)	MR. TOKELEY
Illa	MISS QUANTRELL
Beni ... MASTER HUGHES. Hugo ...	MASTER KEAN
(Children of Kojah and Illa.)	(His first appearance)
Female Savages	MESDMS. WORSDALE, &c., &c.

Tickets to be had of Mr. Kean, at Miss Hake's, feather-maker, No. 211 High Street; of Messrs. Trewman's and Son; and of Mr. Dryer, where places for the boxes may be taken.

Mrs. Buller was in her time and place an illustrious personage, though now her name holds no record in the world's memory. In those days, when a lady favoured a performance with her patronage, it was considered the duty of all friends who wished to stand well in her esteem, of the tradespeople with whom she dealt, and of other vassals to crowd the theatre on the occasion. Kean was therefore to profit by this benefit, for Mrs. Buller's importance was felt by all whose lot it was to live within her sphere. Now her butler, a personage of worth and consideration, one

stout and scant of breath, met the poor player one day
shortly before the night fixed for his benefit, and
heartily congratulated him; "for," said this man of
powder and calves, "you will be sure to have a good
house, as my mistress patronizes the play;" whereon
Kean vowed he would not trouble himself to sell a
single ticket, for if the people didn't come to see his
acting, "it shan't be said they come by Mrs. Buller's
desire." And this tone was the keynote of his conduct.

The hard labour of his professional existence found
no relief in domestic happiness. His home life had little
attraction for him, and his irregularities were many.
Frequently when he was wanted at the theatre he was
found in the tavern, and occasionally it was necessary he
should be taken to the nearest pump, and have his head
douched until, his brains being clear, he was enabled to
play his part; and this being finished, he betook himself
to some orgie where he passed the night. Habits of
dissipation, which eventually ruined his genius and sent
him to a premature grave, now began. For two years he
remained a member of Hughes's company, at the end of
which time he was dismissed. For it happened one night
when he was required, he was found in a condition from
which all contrivances were impossible to immediately
restore him. Hughes was therefore obliged to read his

part; but before the performance concluded Kean made his way into a private box, and in an idiotic state of merriment continually called out at times, when the performance did not warrant such remarks, "Bravo, Hughes, bravo," "Well done, my boy, well done." The play was interrupted, the audience disturbed, and the manager outraged. At the end of the week he was dismissed.

Accompanied by his wife and children he travelled to Portsmouth, and there joined a company crossing to Guernsey; but his career in this island was by no means prosperous. At quite an early period of this engagement he failed to appear on a certain evening when he was announced to play. That a strolling player should dare to disappoint his patrons was a crime the worthy inhabitants could not forgive, and he became unpopular in their eyes. A little weekly publication dignified by the name of a journal makes mention of his acting in phrases amusing to read. "Last night," it stated, "a young man whose name the bills said was Kean made his first appearance as Hamlet, and truly his performance of the character made us wish that we had been indulged with the country system of excluding it, and playing all the other characters. This person has, we understand," continues the critic in a lofty strain, "a high character in several parts of England, and his vanity has repeatedly prompted him to endeavour to procure an engagement at one of the theatres in the metropolis; the difficulties he has met with have, however, proved insurmountable, and the managers of Drury Lane and Covent Garden have saved themselves the disgrace to which they would be subject by countenancing such impudence and incompetency. Even his performance of the inferior characters of the drama would be objectionable, if there was nothing to render him ridiculous but one of the vilest figures that has been seen either on or off the stage; and if his mind was half so qualified for the representation of Richard III., which he is shortly to appear in, as his person is suited to the deformities with which the tyrant is supposed to have been distinguished from his fellows, his success would be most unequivocal. As to his Hamlet, it is one of the most terrible misrepresentations to which Shakespeare has ever been subjected. Without grace or dignity he comes forward; he shows an unconsciousness that anybody is before him, and is often so forgetful of the respect due to an audience that he turns his back upon them in some of those scenes in which contemplation is to be indulged, as if for the purpose of showing his abstractedness from all ordinary subjects. His voice is harsh and monotonous, but as it is deep, answers well enough the idea he entertains of impressing terror by a tone which seems to proceed from a charnel house."

These false and venomous assertions were sufficient to depress the poor player, but other causes for distress remained behind. His salary was a miserable pittance, insufficient to support his family and lodge them, and he relied on his benefit to discharge his debts; but when his benefit night arrived he played to a sparse audience. A day or two later the company departed, but he was unable to leave the island until certain bills were settled. He therefore devised an entertainment, in which he with his wife and eldest boy sang, played, danced, and recited. The Governor of the island, General Sir John Doyle, lent his patronage, and a sufficient sum was realized for Kean to pay his debts and enable him to depart. He and his family soon started for Teignmouth, where they arrived penniless, poorly clad, and downcast.

Here starvation faced them, the darkest hour of many bitter years had arrived ; but his spirit was yet unbroken, and again he had recourse to his talents. Therefore he gave another entertainment in the little sanded floored parlour of a poor inn, charging the modest sum of sixpence admission, and realizing a few shillings, was next morning trudging his weary way towards Exeter. He had friends here who sheltered him until such time as he got an engagement for himself and his wife from Henry Lee, then at Barnstaple, at a joint salary of thirty shillings a week. But now a new grief befel him, for his eldest son, a bright-eyed, golden-haired lad, with winning ways and promising talents, sickened. Lack of food and exposure to cold had told on the delicate constitution of the boy, of whom his father was excessively fond, and he was unable to travel. Under the circumstances necessity compelled the parents to leave Exeter, and Howard was placed for the present in charge of a kindly dressmaker who loved him well.

And now with the autumn of this year, 1813, the turning-point of Kean's fortune was at hand. Whilst at Barnstaple he received a letter from Miss Tidswell, who never forgot his interests, stating she had secured an engagement for him at the Wych Street Theatre, sometimes called Little Drury, and now known as the Olympic, which would soon be opened under the management of Robert William Elliston. Delighted by this news, which came at a time when hope of better days had almost vanished, he wrote the following note to Elliston—

"Barnstaple, Oct. 2, 1813.

"SIR,

"I have this moment received your proposals for the Wych Street Theatre—*id est*—Little Drury. The terms Miss Tidswell, by your authority, mentioned to me are the superintending of the stage, the whole of the principal line of business under all denominations of acting, and an equal division of the house on the night of my benefit, with three guineas a week for salary.

"I place so firm a reliance on your reputed liberality, that on the proof of my humble abilities and assiduity towards the promotion of your interests, you will not be unmindful of mine. I accept, sir, your present proposal, simply requesting you will name what time you expect me in London.

"E. KEAN."

To this came a reply which somewhat damped his hopes. Elliston agreed to engage him for general business, not principal characters; was uncertain when the Wych Street Theatre would open, but bade Kean write to him again a month from the date of his letter, October the 8th, and hoped his engagement would be for their mutual benefit. The dubious tone of this epistle made one over-used to disappointments fear the engagement would never take place, and before the month ended he wrote to Dr. Drury, asking him to exert his influence with the management of Drury Lane towards finding him a place in the company.

Meanwhile the good people of Barnstaple took little interest in the drama, and Manager Lee's company continually played to empty houses. A fresh move was therefore made to Taunton, and after a fortnight spent here, the troop set their faces towards Dorchester. The manager and most of his players set out in advance, and Kean having made a bargain with the owner of a chaise who was returning to a town some thirty miles removed, on the route towards Dorchester, soon followed, accompanied by his wife and child. But they had not travelled far when the conveyance broke down, and its passengers found themselves on the highroad, far removed from any town or hamlet. Upwards of seventy miles lay between them and Dorchester, a distance that now seemed interminable. Kean had just sufficient money in his pocket to buy bread and pay for shelter at night during the days of their journey, and with an unflagging spirit and such cheer as he could assume, he took his boy Charlie upon his back, and set forward on his weary way.

Mile after mile of the dreary road was traversed, and yet it seemed but little advance had been made, because of the distance which lay ahead. The courage which sustained them at morning flagged before night had come, the hours passing silently, their misery being sore. Four brief and bitter winter days came, and they were yet on the road, the young tragedian footsore, cold, hungry, and despairing, his child upon his back ; his wife worn from fatigue, pinched from want, and badly clad, dragging tediously behind, carrying their few belongings wrapped in a bundle, light in itself, but over heavy for her strength. On the evening of this fourth day some faint hope cheered them, for surely their journey must soon be ended. And so they tramped, night falling dark and cheerless over the boundless downs, across which the frosty air swept sadly, penetrating their thin clothes, and chilling their blood, until at last, with straining eyes the miserable outcasts caught sight of faint lights shining here and there, brightening the comfortable hearths and homes of sturdy burghers, and knew they had reached their goal. Entering the High Street, Kean speedily sought his manager, and drawing upon his slender salary in advance, obtained food and refuge for his family.

The theatre opened its doors to the public, bills were

posted on dead walls and freely distributed in shops, but the inhabitants of Dorchester were slow to avail themselves of the treat the player-folk offered. Kean, heartily weary of a stroller's life, and terribly anxious to secure Elliston's engagement, wrote again to the manager, stating that in the event of his services being required before December, he should be ready to make his appearance in Wych Street.

The while he acted as tragedian, comedian, and pantomimist at Dorchester. On the 14th of November, 1813, he, according to previous announcements, played Alexander the Great. The evening was damp and cold. An audience of about twenty persons shivered in the dreary house; oil lamps hung here and there, specks of orange light in general gloom; the footsteps of each new arrival sounded through the theatre. Conversation behind the scenes was audible to those in front. The fiddles in the orchestra squeaked their merriest airs, making believe they were wholly ignorant, or frivolously careless, of the condition of the house, and the consequent suspension of salaries due to their masters. Presently the curtain rose with many a creak, and the tragedy began. The actors, depressed by the sight of unoccupied benches and vacant boxes, carelessly hurried through their parts, their voices sounding unnaturally loud, and awaking echoes in the empty gallery. The tragedy was succeeded by a pantomime farce, for those who paid their money must have its worth; and Kean, who a few minutes before represented a hero of noble sentiments and mighty deeds, now bounded on to the boards in the motley garb of a harlequin. The shivering few in front laughed at his pranks and made merry over his deeds, the while he reviled a fate which caused him to enact the buffoon.

That night whilst washing the paint off his face he was told a gentleman waited to see him; and hurrying on to the stage, he encountered a stranger, who announced himself as Mr. Samuel Arnold, acting manager of Drury Lane Theatre. He stated he had been present during the performance that evening, and requested Kean would come and breakfast with him next morning. Kean was overwhelmed with surprise and apprehension; for remembering the manner in which he had shuffled through his part, he feared all chances of an engagement from Arnold had gone by. Therefore, weighted by gloom, he returned to his wife, saying, " I have ruined myself for ever. Arnold of Drury Lane has been in the house, and I have been gagging and playing carelessly, for who could act to such an audience ? " His faithful,

much-enduring wife gave him some hope by replying,
" It is fortunate you were ignorant of his presence, or
you would have over-acted yourself."

Dr. Drury had on receiving Kean's letter written to
Pascoe Grenfell, M.P., one of the committee of management of Drury Lane, and after some consultation by
the board, it was decided that Arnold, who was regarded
as an excellent critic, should be sent to witness Kean's
performances, and engage him if he proved an actor
of merit. Racked by suspense, alternately elated by
hope and shaken by fear, Kean passed a restless night,
and next morning anxiously waited on the man in
whose power it rested to decide his fate; for now had
the great moment of his life arrived when perchance
the strong desires which had made existence endurable
were about to be realized. The result of his interview
exceeded his expectations. Arnold complimented him
on his acting, and expressed an opinion that he must
succeed upon the London boards. Yet having experience of the unaccountable caprices of the public, he could
not offer him an engagement at a large salary, but
would make him two proposals, either of which he might
accept. He would engage him now, be he successful or
unsuccessful, for three seasons, at eight guineas a week
the first season, nine the second, and ten the third; or

he would pay his expenses to and in London until he made his first appearance, and then if he succeeded, let him make whatever terms he could with the committee; or if not successful, he would defray his expenses back to Dorchester. The character in which he desired to make his first appearance would be left to his own choice, and that he might have a fair struggle for approbation, he would be allowed to play six different parts before a verdict would be pronounced on his merits.

The poor player could scarce believe what he heard was true. An offer of eight guineas a week meant not merely rescue from starvation, but positive wealth, and he eagerly accepted the first proposal. But fearing he had not made a sufficiently strong impression on the manager, Kean begged he would wait and see him play Octavian in *The Mountaineers* that evening; and Arnold complying, his favourable opinion of the actor was confirmed. No mention was made of Elliston.

Surely the hour of the tragedian's triumph was at hand. No more should his family experience the pangs of privations, the humiliations of poverty; no longer need he play harlequin, and laugh and dance whilst his heart ached with pain, and his cheeks flamed with shame; no longer should he strut before sparse audiences of ignorant rustics, to whose mercy he felt indebted for applause; no longer tramp from town to town, a homeless stranger seeking the suffrage of boors. Darkness was about to vanish from his life; he scarce dared look upon the brilliant future which the tardy and longed-for light might reveal. Immediately he expressed his thanks to his kind friend, Dr. Drury, who had written to him and given him advice.

"I have again and again," said Kean in answering, "read your instructive letter, and have each time received additional pleasure from the perusal. Be assured, sir, I shall treasure the admonition it contains *memoria in æternum.* The interview between Mr. Arnold and myself has already passed; that gentleman has honoured me with a visit in Dorchester, the result of which I feel will be as satisfactory to you as liberal and exalted to me. I have competence for three years as a certainty.... I certainly, sir, with submission to your judgment, should be proud to avail myself of the opportunity of paying my devoirs to Mr. Grenfell. Such services I think should be paid by every mark of attention and respect. You have, sir, opened a path of happiness to me so sudden, so unexpected, that I can scarcely think it but a dream. Ita ad hoc ætatis a pueritia fui, ut omnes labores periculo consueta habeam. You have dispelled those clouds and difficulties, and the event, I trust, shall render me deserving of such exalted friendship. In the name of my family, once more I beg you to receive our heartfelt thanks, and believe me, sir, with every deference to your opinions, strict observation to your precepts and example, and continued feelings of gratitude,

"Yours sincerely,

"E. KEAN."

It seemed indeed as if Fate, repentant of the misfortunes long dealt him, had now resolved to repay him, for scarce had Arnold left when Kean received a letter from Elliston, stating that the Wych Street Theatre opened during Christmas week, and he should be glad to see him. To this Kean replied—

"SIR,

"Since I last wrote to you, I have received a very liberal offer from the proprietors of Drury Lane Theatre. It gives me unspeakable regret that the proposals did not reach me before I had commenced negotiating with you; but I hope, sir, you will take a high and liberal view of the question, when I beg to decline the engagement for Little Drury. Another time I shall be happy to treat with you.

"I am, sir,

"Your obedient servant,

"EDMUND KEAN."

Elliston, who was by no means ready to adopt the conduct Kean suggested, called him a deserter, and declared he would "claim his man." With grave misgivings Kean prepared for his journey to London, but before leaving Dorchester news reached him that his oldest son was dead. This was a blow for which he was unprepared, and coming on the eve of his triumph, thrust him back into depression and grief. "The joy I felt three days since at my flattering prospects of future prosperity," he writes to Dr. Drury, "is now obliterated by the unexpected loss of my child. Howard, sir, died on Monday morning last. You may conceive my feelings."

But even in the midst of his sorrow he was obliged to continue his performances at the Dorchester Theatre, that he might support himself, and secure his right to a benefit, the proceeds of which he trusted would defray his expenses to town. He now played in tragedies with no need to simulate grief, and acted in comedies with a merry face and a sad heart; but when his benefit night came the house was almost empty, and the necessary funds not forthcoming from the treasury, he borrowed five pounds from manager Lee, and leaving his wife and son at Dorchester until he should be able to send for them, he, with mingled feelings of hope and fear, regret and rejoicement, set out for the capital.

CHAPTER IV.

ARRIVING in London towards the close of dull
November, Kean sought lodgings at 21 Cecil Street,
Strand, and in due time presented himself to Arnold,
who received him with signs of hearty pleasure and
words of kindly welcome. From that hour he told
Kean his engagement began, and a date would speedily
be fixed for his first appearance. His fears were now
at rest, the more so because he heard an acting
manager for the Wych Street Theatre had been engaged
by Elliston, and he therefore trusted no further trouble
would be given him.

On the following Saturday he presented himself at the treasury office of Drury Lane Theatre, and received his first week's salary; the greater part of this he sent to his wife, that she and Charles might join him, which was accordingly done. He was now in buoyant spirits, believing the hardships of life to rest far behind him, and with bright dreams of success in the future, looking ardently forward to the first night when he should tread the boards of the national theatre. At the close of the second week he again claimed his salary, but to his great astonishment and bitter disappointment, it was boldly refused him. Hoping, nay, believing some mistake had been made, he sought the manager, but his unfriendly looks and cold glances filled Kean with apprehension; he indignantly stated Elliston had assured him Kean was engaged for the Wych Street Theatre, and therefore the matter must be settled with him before Kean could consider himself a member of the Drury Lane company.

Robert William Elliston, the son of a watchmaker, had been intended for the Church. But falling in with a school-boy named Charles Mathews, the son of a bookseller, a lively lad given to reciting and acting, he and Elliston became friends, and together joined

an amateur company. The stage exercised such an
attraction for young Elliston, that when only sixteen
he ran away to Bath, at the theatre of which city he
obtained an engagement; and now at the age of forty
he was one of the most notable men in the theatrical
profession. An actor no less off than on the stage, his
manner was bland and winning towards those he wished
to attract or conciliate, but brusque and harsh to all
he desired to punish or subdue. Active, bustling, and
loquacious, his wit was the theme of green-rooms,
whilst his conduct frequently outstepped eccentricity.
He was at once a fine comedian and a delightful
companion, altogether, as Charles Lamb styled him,
" a pleasant creature."

At this period he was lessee and manager of the
Surrey and Olympic Theatres, on the stages of which,
as well as that of Drury Lane, he continually played,
having from the latter house a salary of thirty pounds
a week for three nights' performances weekly. As a
manager he was an excellent business man, and from
his love of governing many theatres at once, was styled
" the Napoleon of the stage." The actors he engaged
for his town houses were generally made to divide
their labour between each every evening. The Surrey
and the Olympic lie far apart, the Thames running

between; and frequently when some poor player with a salary of fifteen shillings a week had caused roars of laughter at one theatre, he hastened to repeat his performance at the other; so that for those crossing Blackfriars Bridge at night, it was no uncommon sight to see a brace of half-clad players, with painted faces and shivering limbs, trot in the splashing mud behind some galloping coach, which they, fresh from a warm atmosphere, used as a shelter from cold winds or pelting rain; anxiety strong within them that they were not behind time for their parts.

An incident which justly illustrates Elliston's character happened shortly after Kean's arrival in town. The manager had dismissed from the Olympic company one Carles, an excellent actor, a great favourite with his audiences, whose only fault was that of "taking a drop too much." Learning of his dismissal, his patrons, who knew nothing of him save that he was a clever player, rallied round him, and in powerful numbers sallied into the Olympic pit, determined on having their hero reinstated. · Carles sat in their midst awaiting the proceedings which were soon to begin; for no sooner was the curtain raised than loud cries rang through the house for the manager. On Elliston's appearance he was greeted with universal shouts of "Carles, Carles! engage Carles! let's have Carles! Carles or no play!"

Elliston, perfectly cool, faced the storm, with his hand upon his heart and a smile on his lips, and when silence was granted him, began with a touch of pathos in his voice, "My best, my warmest friends, this ebullition of feeling in behalf of one you suppose to have been wronged shows the nobleness of your nature, and I adore you for it. The man who would hesitate to stretch forth his utmost might to rescue from the bitter fangs of oppression the object of tyranny and persecution, is unworthy to enjoy the blessings of that liberty for which our forefathers fought and bled." Loud applause from all parts of the house. "I loved that man," continued this diverting humbug, pointing to Carles in the pit, "oh, I loved him; I idolized his transcendent talent, and took him to my heart like a brother. To my poor thinking he appeared the moving picture of all that could adorn humanity; he would, to be sure, get a little tipsy sometimes, but I always looked upon it as an amiable weakness. We all get tipsy sometimes; I do." Here a general titter rippled through the audience at this candid confession of a well-known fact. Elliston had his hearers with him, and he now came to the pith of his discourse.

"But for the last week," he said, glancing again at
Carles, "he has been in a continued state of intoxi-
cation, and has never been near the theatre." Carles
rose from his seat to protest, but was greeted with
shouts, "Down in front! hats off! down in front!"
The tide had turned, and poor Carles sat down, whilst
Elliston continued hurriedly—"And on going to his
lodgings this morning, that I might coax him to return
as I have often done before, judge of my horror and
astonishment, when I found his wife and children
starving for the want of common necessaries of life!"
Here a voice in the gallery shouted, "Carles hasn't got
no wife;" to which a universal cry went up, "Pitch him
over." Then Elliston proceeded—"His lawfully-wedded
wife, the loveliest, thin young creature I ever beheld,
whom this villain had torn from her fond, gray-haired
father's arms to bring her to misery and leave her to
perish for want; the infant at her breast screaming for
the nourishment the starving mother couldn't give;
the little ones, four lovely boys, clasping my knees and
shrieking for bread; and in the corner of the room lay
his infant daughter, the most lovely angel from heaven I
ever beheld, a frightful distorted corpse, too horrible to
look upon, who the day before had died for want of
food." A general murmur of indignation swept through

the house, but Elliston went on—"I instantly sent for food for the little ones, and with the sum this villain could easily have earned, I provided a coffin for the little cherub, and only half an hour ago I returned from the funeral. Now I appeal to you as men, as husbands, and as fathers, should I engage this inhuman monster? if so, he shall instantly be reinstated."

Poor Carles, bewildered by the tissue of lies he had just heard, rose to say he had neither wife nor child, but the infuriated audience cried, "Out with him!" "Knock him over!" "Monster!" and those nearest laying vengeful hands upon him, he, not without some injuries, escaped from their anger, whilst Elliston was loudly applauded and heartily praised.

From a man of this complexion Kean could expect little mercy, and when Arnold assured him he must set himself right with him, the poor player left Drury Lane with a heavy heart. The remainder of the day was spent by him in seeking Elliston at his theatres, at his home, at his various haunts, but his search was vain; and weary, dispirited, and penniless he returned at night to his family. After some consideration he wrote Elliston the following note, which he hoped might move him to his desires—

" SIR,

"The fate of my family is in your hands. Are you determined to crush the object that never injured you? In one word, are you to receive our imprecations or our blessings?

"Through your means I am deprived of my situation in Drury Lane Theatre, unless I produce a document from you that I am not a member of the new Olympic. How can you reconcile this more than Turkish barbarity? If you must display your power, direct it against one more fortunate than myself. You have become a thorn in the side of my young fortune. I shall conclude by simply requesting you to inform me whether I am to become a member of the Theatre Royal, Drury Lane, or again, penniless, hopeless, and despised, am I to be cast on the provinces, the rejected of this great city, which should afford a home to industry of every kind? With my family at my back will I return, for the walls of Wych Street I will never enter. In this strong determination, but with weakened respect for you, sir, I am,

"E. KEAN."

In answer to this letter Elliston said—

"To any man with the smallest gift of intellect and

the dimmest sense of honour, it must appear that on the 11th of November, and previous to that time, you deemed yourself engaged to me, and that subsequently a more attractive offer having been made, you held it convenient to consider a pledge as idle words muttered in a dream. All my engagements are made and fulfilled with honour on my part, and I expect an equal punctuality from others.

"R. W. ELLISTON."

This note brought no hope, but Kean was determined he would never submit to Elliston. Meanwhile he daily waited at Drury Lane Theatre, loitering about the doors, or sitting in the porter's room, seeking an opportunity of seeing Arnold, to whom he wished to explain his position more fully; but if by accident he encountered that personage, he merely frowned upon him and refused to give him an audience.

It seemed as if he were now as far removed from his anticipated triumph as he had been months ago; but hardships and poverty had not broken his spirit in the past, neither should disappointment nor neglect overwhelm him in the present. The courage inseparable from genius supported him. Much need had he for endurance, for he was sorely tried. The players passing to morning rehearsals or evening performances looked askance at the dark-complexioned, bright-eyed little man, clad in a rough gray coat with large capes; and aware of his purpose, regarded him as one who presumed to usurp their rights. The slights and insults he received from many of them were bitter. Rae, now playing tragedy in this house, passed him in the hall without deigning to notice him. Munden recommended him to "Spend his evenings in front, trying to improve himself by witnessing the performances of good actors;" a lady of some merit wondered "where the little wretch had been picked up," and eventually advised him to "return to the country, for amongst such actors as surrounded him in London, he could have no chance;" whilst the company generally spoke of him as "Arnold's hard bargain."

Sensitive and proud, he shrank from them, but though mortified and humiliated, he was not yet subdued. "Let me once set my foot before the floats, and I'll let them see what I am," he said to his wife; and she, poor soul, believing in him with firm faith, and loving him with strong affection, was heavily weighted by anxiety and suspense she strove to conceal, lest it might add to his burden. "Ah, sir," she said subsequently to a friend, "the Drury Lane folks only looked at his little body, they did not know what he could do with his eye."

His position seemed hopeless. "My dear Lee," he wrote to his late manager, "I am in a damned situation, or rather, in no situation at all. Elliston has claimed my services, but I will never join him. The Drury Lane committee have decided against me, and have actually withdrawn my salary. Not all the world or the world's ills shall force me into Wych Street. So here am I in London, without friends, without money, and a brand upon me by which I can acquire neither."

Days came and went, and yet Kean's prospects remained in the same position. After some further correspondence with Elliston, he had a personal interview with him in the presence of Arnold. The latter was still wrathful with him for not having mentioned during their interview at Dorchester that he had entered into negotiations with the manager of Wych Street, and now assured him he stood most unfavourably in his estimation. Kean would have explained, but Elliston, loud-voiced and demonstrative, by his extreme volubility overwhelmed him, and beat down his words, so that Kean was obliged to listen submissively. The meeting ended without any decision having been arrived at;

but before they parted, Arnold told Kean if he acted at any other theatre than that of Drury Lane he could enter an action against him.

A month had now almost passed since the poor player had arrived in town, and with the exception of the eight pounds he received from the Drury Lane treasury, which had gone to defray his wife's expenses to town, he had received no money. For days they starved, and would have needed shelter, but for the charity of their landlady, Miss Williams, who in return for apologies for non-payment gave words of hope. " There is something about Mr. Kean," she told his wife, " which tells me he will be a great man." At last Kean's private circumstances becoming known to Miss Mellon, through Oxberry, an actor with whom he had of yore shared a stroller's privations, this good-hearted woman resolved to help him. Therefore it happened that one day whilst Mrs. Kean, distressed by hunger and harassed by fears, sat with her boy in the garret she dared not call her own, Miss Mellon's companion called and placed a packet in her hands, which she said came from an anonymous donor. On opening it the distressed wife found it contained a sum sufficient to keep starvation at bay some time longer.

The bleak and bitter days of December wore slowly

by, bringing no change to Kean in their passage. About a week from his last interview with Elliston he waited on him, and, to his great surprise, found him in a conciliatory humour. The manager declared he had resolved to relinquish all claim to his services, but would ask him in return to play at his theatre in Birmingham during the summer vacation. Poor Kean regarded this as a compliment, and promising to comply with his desires hastened to seek Arnold. After some delay he was admitted to the presence of the great man, who stated that an actor from Drury Lane had been sent to take his place at the Wych Street Theatre, and in consequence he must pay his salary of two pounds a week. Anxious to have his engagement settled at any cost, Kean made no objection, and asked if he might apply again at the treasury for his week's salary; but Arnold informed him he must first obtain from Elliston a written statement that he held him no longer engaged.

The day following was Friday, Christmas Eve, and Kean, doubtful of the humour in which he might find Elliston, and fearful lest he might not accede to his request, set out in search for him. From ten o'clock in the morning until three in the afternoon he continued his quest, and only at the last-mentioned hour was the busy, bustling manager found at the Surrey Theatre, where he wrote the acknowledgment required. With this in his hand Kean, already footsore and weary, hastened across Blackfriars Bridge, and arriving at Drury Lane asked to see the manager, but was informed Mr. Arnold could not see him then; he therefore sent in his name. "For nearly one hour," Kean wrote to Dr. Drury, describing the events of this day, "I waited in the passage with the rest of the menials of the theatre, had the mortification of seeing them all conducted to his presence before myself, and when summoned at last to appear, was, with the continued brow of severity, informed that I had no claim upon the treasurers. My engagement had all to begin again. I shall not forget the day of the month. I returned to my family penniless. At a period when everybody appeared happy at the celebration of the time, our fates appeared clouded and miserable. Your letter of the 23rd reached me on Monday; and I forgot my cares in the hopes of seeing you, and perhaps forgetting my disagreeables by the public favour—the balmy cordial that heals all actors' sorrows. Judge if possible my disappointed hopes on seeing another person advertised for the very character on which I built my fame. Was this fair dealing?

I cannot define justice if it was. Necessity again draws me to the treasury to-day; and I doubt not but I shall return with some additional mortification."

The other person to whom he referred was an actor named Huddart from Dublin, who now made his first appearance at Drury Lane as Shylock, the character in which Kean intended to make his *début*. Fortunately for the latter, Huddart was a signal failure, and the Othello of Sowerby, seen five nights later, shared the same fate. Yet no effort was made to bring Kean forward. Dr. Drury besought him to "bear all; bear all, only come out;" whilst Whitbread, the chairman of the Drury Lane committee, to whom Kean addressed himself, replied with solid wisdom, that if he had talent he would be able to show it on his appearance, if not he must return to the country; but concerning his misunderstanding with the manager, he knew nothing.

The affairs of Drury Lane Theatre were at this period managed, or rather mismanaged, by a committee of shareholders; from which was formed a sub-committee of management, numbering Lord Essex, Lord Byron, the Hon. George Lamb, the Hon. Douglas Kinnaird, and Mr. Peter Moore. Under their direction the national theatre had fallen into disrepute. The pieces selected for production, and the actors engaged to perform, had failed to attract; the coffers were empty, and the gloomiest fears regarding the future were generally entertained. Huddart and Sowerby having failed, it was decided to give the little man from Dorchester a chance. Therefore towards the end of January he had the honour of being summoned before the council assembled, and entered their presence calm, self-contained, resolute, prepared for any decision at which the committee might arrive. His stature—five feet five inches—and his general appearance led them to doubt his possessing the attractions for which Arnold had formerly vouched, and it was therefore proposed he should test public appreciation by appearing in a character of secondary importance.

This suggestion he heard in silence, and then fixing his eyes steadily on the chairman, said he would play lead or nothing. He reminded his hearers that a choice of characters had been guaranteed him on his engagement, and he claimed the fulfilment of this promise. His earnestness and determination conquered; it was agreed that he should act Shylock on the 26th of the month. Though he had triumphed over the difficulties which beset him, his trials had not yet ended. The solitary advertisement in the *Times*, that on

Wednesday Mr. Kean of the Theatre Royal, Exeter, would make his first appearance at Drury Lane in the character of Shylock, in the *Merchant of Venice*, caused little interest and less excitement, his name being unknown. At the first rehearsal few of the cast were present, excuses being sent for those absent. One lady wrote to deplore her inability to leave home because, as she elegantly explained, she had "got such a headache as never was." In some scenes only Kean and Thomas Dibdin, who then acted as prompter at the theatre, were on the stage. "I apologized to Mr. Kean," says Dibdin, "for this seeming neglect, which he appeared quite indifferent about." At later rehearsals, when the company attended, their presence was not more satisfactory than their absence to the new actor. Scene after scene was gone through in a desultory and spiritless manner, the men sulky and stern, the fairer members saucy and flippant. Once when Kean accompanied a speech by some unconventional act, George Raymond, the stage manager, stopped him.

"That will never do," he said. "It is an innovation, sir, and totally different from anything that has been done on these boards."

Kean regarded him calmly before replying—

"Sir, I wish it to be so."

"But," said Bustling Raymond, as he was generally called, "it will not do, be assured of that."

"Well, sir," answered Kean, "perhaps I may be wrong, but if so the public will set me right."

When not required upon the stage he stood apart silent and observing. At such times remarks were made by those around, doubtless with a design that he should hear them, but to outward seeming he paid no heed. One wondered how Arnold could have engaged him; another asked when would the committee cease to trifle with the public; a third felt certain the little man must soon return to the obscurity from which he sprang; a fourth mimicked the peculiarities of his voice midst roars of laughter. On Kean, who, as he said of himself, could see a sneer across Salisbury Plain, these remarks were not lost; but he who had borne much had strength to endure more.

Long years after he told Joe Cowen the comedian, that one day Miss Tidswell was so provoked by the general ridicule flung upon him, that in the middle of a scene she came forward and poked him in the back with her umbrella, and beckoning him to one of the wings, urged him not to persevere in his intentions of acting, for the players, all of whom were good judges and experienced men, were laughing at him; and she begged him to consider how horrible the disgrace of his being "pelted from the stage would be to her." When the rehearsal was finished that day he left the theatre weighed down by depression, for even his own friend had no faith in him. But he had not gone many steps when he encountered an old comrade who had starved and strolled with him in the provinces. To him Kean unburdened his heart, with its load of hopes and fears, and in return received encouragement to face the dreadful odds that seemed to overwhelm him. And this friend having five shillings, the sole sum he possessed, and both being hungry, they repaired to a neighbouring tavern, enjoyed a dinner, and drank a pot of porter. Then by degrees Kean's dreams of success and scorn of those who mocked him returned fourfold. For observation of the world had shown him that were he successful the manner of all men would change towards him; that they who sneered at him now would fawn upon him then; that those who ignored him to-day would boast him their friend to-morrow. Therefore the pettiness and malice of his fellow-players was lost sight of in the strong hope of triumph, dimly foreseen through years of darkness, and awaited with eagerness unabated by distress.

At last the day dawned on which he was to make his appearance at Drury Lane, Friday the 26th of January, 1814. The memorable frost of this year had set in with the first days of the month. Snow lay thick upon the streets, and was shovelled into huge white banks at the corners. Traffic on foot through pathways of trampled black slush was dangerous, and by vehicle almost impossible. In many parts the Thames was completely frozen over; between Blackfriars Bridge and London Bridge a fair was held upon the ice, on which booths were erected, bands played, printing presses worked, and the people eat, drank, and made merry. On the 26th of January a sheep was roasted whole on the frozen river between the bridges of Hammersmith and Putney, and then divided amongst the poor of the parish. The weather was such as to incline mankind to remain within their warm homes at night, rather than seek the usually cheerless aspect of bare benches and empty boxes at Drury Lane Theatre.

The short afternoon hours of the bitter winter day wore to gloomy eve, and every moment carried Kean nearer to the hour of his trial, ardently longed-for in the past, nervously dreaded in the present. He had dined that day, for he needed strength, and then impatiently waited the time when he should start.

Occasionally his hopes surmounted his fears, and thinking of all that had been in the past, with what might be in the future, he muttered, "If I succeed I shall go mad." Towards six o'clock he wrapped himself in his rough coat of many capes, and with Shylock's costume in a bundle under his arm, left his garret, his wife's tremulous words of encouragement and hope ringing in his ears as he took his slow way through the silent, snow-covered streets to Drury Lane. Arriving at the theatre, he was conducted to the place allotted him as a dressing-room, but this being unsuitable to his requirements, he went to the supernumeraries' apartment, and there donned the Jewish gaberdine.

A thin, scattered audience in the pit betrayed neither excitement nor impatience; an array of empty boxes faced the stage; the noise of a half-filled gallery and the music of the orchestra sounded with a distinctness betraying a cheerless house. One of the players looking through a rent in the curtain, announced to his fellows, with an air not wholly devoid of satisfaction, "there was a shy domus," to which another replied, "What do you expect? there'll be nothing until half-price;" indicating that the attraction of the evening would be the afterpiece, a farce called *The Apprentice*, in which Jack Bannister played.

Presently the curtain rose, and the play began. Rac, dogged and indifferent, entered as Bassanio and spoke his speeches; and soon the prompter gave the call-boy notice to summon Shylock. The lad hastened to the apartment which had been allotted to Kean, but not finding him, rushed to the green-room; he was not there. Alarmed at this, the boy was hurrying back to report the fact, when he saw Kean waiting at the wing where he was to make his entrance.

"You're called, sir," he said, breathless from excitement.

"Thank you," replied Kean; and these were the only words, save those of Shakespeare, which he spoke whilst he remained in the theatre that night.

The hour destined to decide his fate had come, and by the power he wielded must his future be bright or black. As he entered on the scene with Bassanio he was received with applause, which was rather cordial than enthusiastic, to which he bowed slightly, and then began his part. His fine, intellectual face, the brilliancy of his eyes, and the resonant tones of his voice impressed the house favourably; but silence was maintained until, on the exit of Bassanio, he spoke the lines—

> "If I can catch him once upon the hip,
> I will feed fat the ancient grudge I bear him,"

when he was warmly applauded. Then by the magnetic feeling which passes from audience to actor, he felt he had gained a hold upon his hearers; knew, as he long afterwards expressed himself, he had them with him. Encouragement aided him; his enthusiasm kindled, his efforts increased, his power strengthened. The taunting speeches of Shylock were spoken with delicacy and poignancy, his pauses were just and effective, the dexterity with which he modulated his voice excellent; and when the curtain fell on the first act, welcome applause sounded in his ears.

The company when not engaged with him in the scenes had stood at the wings to watch him, and now on returning to the green-room the chief comment made was, "I say, he has got a black wig and beard; did you ever see Shylock in a black wig?" Still Kean kept apart from them, avoiding the green-room, wandering up and down at the back of the stage whilst the orchestra played, and the scenes of the second act, in which Shylock does not appear, were performed. The house was now fairly filled, for a new comic opera, entitled *A Farmer's Wife*, being advertised for a first performance at Covent Garden, and withdrawn at the last moment, many of those disappointed by the change in the bill crossed over to see the new tragedian at Drury Lane.

Again he was ready in his place when the call-boy would have summoned him, and the breathless silence with which his words were listened to assured him of the growing influence he gained over his audience; nor did it decrease whilst he played. Now and then the heartily-expressed approbation he received gave fresh energy to his tones, new fire to his eyes, increased expression to his gestures; and such was the force and intelligence of the latter, that one might say, as the *Examiner* remarked, "his body thought."

At the beginning of the third act the players seated in the green-room were startled by the sounds of stormy applause, and asking each other what it could be, they hastened to the wings, and saw Shylock raging like a lion in the scene with Tubal; his voice, eyes, actions, and expressions were pregnant with meaning. The house was now fairly roused to excitement, and again and again its appreciation was so forcibly expressed, that Oxberry said, "How the devil so few of them kicked up such a row was marvellous." Especially in the trial scene was he warmly applauded, and then, his part being ended, he quickly changed his clothes and quietly left the theatre before the play had concluded.

One who witnessed his playing that night, and

regarded it as a revelation, beheld in it "the first gleam of genius breaking athwart the gloom of the stage." This was William Hazlitt, the dramatic critic of the *Morning Chronicle*. In this paper he published the first words which heralded Kean's greatness. "In giving effect to the conflict of passions arising out of the contrast of situation," he wrote of Kean, "in varied. vehemence of declamation, in keenness of sarcasm, in the rapidity of his transitions from one tone or feeling to another, in propriety and novelty of action, presenting a succession of striking pictures, and giving perpetually fresh shocks of delight and surprise, it would be difficult to single out a competitor. The fault of his acting was (if we may hazard an objection) an over display of the resources of his art, which gave too much relief to the hard, impenetrable, dark ground-work of Shylock. It would be needless to point out individual beauties, when almost every passage was received with equal and deserved applause. His style of acting is, if we may use the expression, more significant, more pregnant with meaning, more varied and alive in every part, than any we have almost ever witnessed. The character never stands still; there is no vacant pause in the action; the eye is never silent. It is not saying too much of Mr. Kean, though it is saying a great deal, that he is all that Mr. Kemble wants of perfection."

The *Morning Post* briefly commented on his marked and expressive countenance, his deep, sonorous voice, his mastery of his art; but neither the eulogies of these papers, nor the applause of those who witnessed his acting, convinced those in connection with the theatre that he possessed unusual talent, not to mention genius. One of the company said that to compare him with Charles Young (a poor, mechanical actor) was ridiculous; whilst a player who was deputed by the Covent Garden management to report on the merits " of the new man at the Lane," declared " the play had gone well enough, but he couldn't do,"—this gentleman's judgment being fully on a level with his power of expression. Had the managers known the ability Kean possessed, and would shortly exercise to fill their coffers, they would not, now the theatre was on the verge of bankruptcy, have allowed almost a week to pass between his first and second performances.

His second appearance, after an interval of five days, was brought about by accident, as Thomas Dibdin records. Although, he says, the judicious few approved Kean's acting, " but little notice was taken of it either in or out of the theatre; and for a few days scarcely

anything was said respecting him. A necessary but
unexpected change of play on some occasion caused the
usual question, What shall we act? from the stage
manager; I immediately advised a second appearance
of 'the new gentleman.' Mr. Raymond said that was
also Mr. Arnold's wish, and Mr. Kean played Shylock
again on the first, third, and fifth of February."

On each of his succeeding performances the house
became more and more crowded; his power seemed
likewise to increase. Douglas Jerrold used to say that
from the moment Kean entered as Shylock and leaned
upon his stick, listening gravely to the request made
him for monies, he impressed his audience "like a
chapter of Genesis." On the first night he had played,
the sum taken at the doors merely amounted to one
hundred and sixty-four pounds; on the evening of his
second appearance the treasury held more than double
that sum, and for the fourteen nights during which he
represented Shylock this season, the receipts reached
four thousand nine hundred and twenty-one pounds
three shillings. Every time his performance was
repeated, his originality, study, and ability were more
perceptible; flashes of genius lighted passages rendered
obscure by other actors; touches of nature made him
akin with his hearers; his power swayed his audiences

at will. To one who had stood on the brink of hope, and been swept back into the blackness of despair, triumph was at last assured.

And yet those who acted with him were slow to admit his genius, though glad for sake of their salaries he was able to crowd the house whenever he played. This fact was, however, set down by them as a craze from which the town suffered—a whim that would pass in a day or a week. Master Betty had created a greater sensation in his time, and John Kemble was for a while overlooked; this provincial stroller, with his new-fangled ways, would doubtless in a little while share Master Betty's ultimate fate, and sink into obscurity, when the John Kembles of Drury Lane would shine in their proper spheres. "God renounce me," said old Dowton gruffly, as he sat in the green-room whilst Kean was playing Shylock for the fifth time, " 'tis only necessary now-a-days to be under four feet high, have bandy legs and a hoarseness, and mince my liver, but you'll be thought a great tragedian."

"Nay," said Munden, a fellow player, knowing to whom Dowton referred; "no doubt the little man has great powers of entertainment, for I hear he's a wonderful tumbler."

"Of that," replied Jack Bannister, "there can be

no doubt, for he has jumped over the heads of us all."

Miss Mellon differed in her opinion from those around her, for she believed in his future greatness. On the morning of his first performance Oxberry, Kean's friend, had, at her request, introduced him to her. Kean's manner on that occasion being shy and reserved, made her fear he would resent her friendliness as intrusion; but on meeting him at the conclusion of his third performance she congratulated him on his success, and predicted his brilliant future. At the same time, she inquired if he had signed his agreement with the managers, and on his replying he had not, she begged he would defer doing so until his position was more secure, when he would be certain to receive much better terms. On this subject, however, Kean had his ideas of honour, and when summoned before the committee soon after, and handed for signature a contract of an engagement for three years, at an increasing salary of eight, nine, and ten pounds weekly, he affixed his name to it without hesitation. The chairman then taking it from him tore it, and presented a second form, guaranteeing him twenty pounds a week, which he requested him to sign. Moreover, the management gave him fifty guineas, probably hoping

this gift would induce Kean to overlook the humiliations and vexations to which he had recently been
subjected.

And having played Shylock for six nights to large
and enthusiastic audiences, the committee were anxious
he should represent another character. Dibdin suggested Richard III., but many voices were raised
against his wish. Kean was desirous of acting this
his favourite character, and eventually the committee
consented that he should appear as the crook-backed
king. It was felt that this character, so widely different
from that of Shylock, would greatly test his powers,
and the town was on the tip-toe of expectation. The
management took unusual interest in the revival;
rehearsals were frequent; new scenery, archæologically
and historically correct, was painted for the occasion.
The while Kean's manner was as reserved and un-
obtrusive as when he had first appeared on the stage
of Drury Lane; nay, he was even willing to accept
suggestions from those he fancied might be able to
guide him aright.

During the rehearsals he gave no indications of how
he really meant to play when before the public; but
hearing him mutter certain passages, Dibdin considered they were not in accordance with his own ideas

as to the manner in which they should be uttered; and as Miss Tidswell had requested him to be free and candid in his opinions of Kean's representation, the prompter when alone with the new actor spoke his mind. Kean, who had previously declined to follow the stage-manager's suggestion roughly given before the company, now listened to the man he believed to be his friend. He therefore asked Dibdin, as a favour, to take his copy of *Richard III.* home, and write his comments on the speeches to which he referred. When the prompter complied with his request he received them, writes Dibdin, " with every appearance of pleasure, and at the next rehearsal paid me the compliment of apparently adopting every suggestion; though I am now convinced that the errors I had ventured to correct had been merely the effect of a careless indifference with which he almost unconsciously rehearsed."

The date of the performance was fixed for Saturday the 12th of February (1814). For more than a week previously every box in the theatre was engaged, and on the afternoon of this day the pit and gallery doors were besieged by eager throngs. Before six o'clock Drury Lane was blocked by the carriages of the most famous men and women of the age. Excitement and expectation reigned within the theatre; the new tragedian was the theme of every tongue; gossip false and true regarding his early life, speculation concerning his future career, echoes of the green-room anent his personality, were freely exchanged and repeated. Behind the scenes the same atmosphere of feverish anticipation prevailed. Members of the committee, the stage and acting managers, passed and repassed behind the curtain, where the great murmur of the crowded audience was audible; the prompter, impressed by the importance of the occasion, gave orders in a nervous voice; supernumeraries stood in groups; scene-shifters were yet at work, and a crowd of distinguished visitors went to and from Kean's dressing-room, now a handsome apartment lined with mirrors. Here, whilst Lord Essex, Douglas Kinnaird, Whitbread, and Raymond stood watching him as he attired himself in the gorgeous costume of the Duke of Gloucester, and practised gestures before the glass, Frederick Reynolds the dramatist, with solemn face and uplifted finger, cried, " Hush, do not disturb him."

The orchestra finished the overture, but the curtain did not rise; instead, Wroughton, one of the actors, came forward, and for a second fear held all breathless, and the question rose in each mind, had Kean been taken suddenly ill; but they were soon set at rest.

Wroughton merely expressed a hope all present would excuse the hoarseness from which Mr. Kean suffered; his reluctance to disappoint his patrons alone induced him to appear before them that evening. Another second, and the curtain rose; all eyes were fixed on the stage to behold Kean enter. His dark-complexioned face was pale from excitement, his eyes were lustrous with anticipated triumph. His appearance was the signal for a great outburst of welcome; then in a moment the house was hushed, and the play began.

The low tones of his voice fell like music on the ears of his hearers as he spoke the opening soliloquy, the mere action of pointing with his finger at himself when complaining of being

> " Scarce half made up,
> And that so lamely and unfashionable
> That dogs bark at me as I halt by them,"

caused a round of applause that interrupted his speech, and by the time he had finished it was agreed by all present a great actor stood before them. In the scene with the Lady Anne, " an enchanting smile played upon his lips, while a courteous humility bowed his head. His voice, though hoarse from cold, was yet modulated to a tone which no common female mind ever did or could resist. Gentle yet self-respecting, insinuating yet determined, humble yet over-awing, he presented an object by which the mere human senses must from their very constitution be subjected and entranced." His attitude in leaning against the side of the stage in this scene was so graceful and striking, that Hazlitt considered him a subject worthy of Titian's brush.

It would be impossible to enumerate the countless beauties of his performance, but all present carried away remembrances of the manner in which he, when taunted by the little Duke of York, conveyed the idea of rage stifled beneath a calm exterior; as well as his air whilst listening to the entreaties of the Lord Mayor that he would be king. When Buckingham demands what shall be done if Hastings prove cold to their design, the prompt decision of a mind which never hesitated concerning the removal of those who obstructed his purpose, was admirably conveyed in the quick, abrupt manner of his reply, "Chop off his head." The activity of his mind, visible in his expressive face, held his audience spell-bound. He had set aside the stale traditions of the stage, ignored the methods of other players past and present, and marked his performance with the stamp of originality.

As the play continued his power increased. When on bidding his friends good night, whilst he drew the

point of his sword backwards and forwards slowly and
meditatively, his action seemed so just, graceful, and
natural that the whole house loudly expressed its
admiration. His exit when retiring to his tent was
declared by the critic of the *Morning Post* " one of the
finest pieces of acting we have ever beheld, or perhaps
that the stage has ever known." But the concluding
scene was the most brilliant of all, producing an effect
of unequalled power and grandeur. Here his skill as
a fencer served him well ; before allowing himself to
be killed upon Bosworth battle-field, he chased Rae,
who played Richmond, round and round the stage,
whilst steel clashed, and the excitement to which he
had gradually worked his audience rose to a climax ;
then stumbling, he recovered himself quickly, still
fighting " like one drunk with wounds," continuing
even after he had lost his sword and received his death-
blow to thrust at his adversary with his empty hand, as if
his indomitable spirit would be overcome by death alone.

His death scene, the *Examiner* remarked, " was a
piece of noble poetry, expressed by action instead of
language." As the curtain fell the audience rose as one
man, cheered lustily, applauded wildly, declaring by
word and action this new actor was great indeed. For
the first time he now felt assured of success above and

beyond all doubt and disappointment, and returning to his home in Cecil Street that night, he told his wife of the crowds that had gathered to see him, the applause which greeted him, the fervour that possessed him. "I could not," he said, "feel the stage under me." Then he dwelt on the coming time. "Our fortune is made, and you shall ride in your carriage, and my boy shall go to Eton." For a second came a shadow from the past, and he paused. "If only Howard had lived," he said sadly, but quickly added, "yet he is better where he is." And in present triumph past pain was forgotten.

Verily his fame was now established, nor were signs wanting of his success. Men of fashion and distinction, peers and poets, artists and dramatists, were anxious to congratulate him; the committee became solicitous regarding his cold; the papers were full of his praise. "We cannot imagine," says the *Morning Chronicle*, "any character represented with greater distinctness and precision, more perfectly articulated in every part. Perhaps, indeed, there is too much of this, for we sometimes thought he failed even from an exuberance of talent, and dissipated the impressions of the character by the variety of his resources; but in one who dares so much there is little indeed to blame." The

Examiner could not recollect any performance, the very finest exhibition of Mrs. Siddons not excepted, which was so calculated to delight an audience, and impress it with veneration for the talents of an actor. Even the *Times*, which had spoken of his Shylock in phrases of petty patronage intermingled with mild censure, now commended him in a genteel and paltry manner. That he possessed powers of mind was obvious in the judgment with which he marked and discriminated many difficult passages. He gave several parts with propriety, but was not equally fortunate " in the loftier doings of the heroic," whatever they may be. He disappointed no reasonable expectation; he was a young man, and considering he had not a very great experience of the stage, his ease and self-possession were commendable. This journal finally admitted, that scarcely ever was heard " greater applause than this young man received during the play, and especially at its conclusion."

The committee of Drury Lane marked their admiration by presenting him with one hundred guineas; Lord Essex gave him a handsome sword; and Mr. Whitbread, calling one day on Mrs. Kean, took her boy Charles on his knee, and put a fifty-pound note into the lad's hands.

The cold Kean had contracted increased during the

days succeeding his exertion, and hæmorrhage ensued, followed by feverish symptoms. The committee, now careful of a life that had become important to their fortunes, sent Dr. Parson, one of the most famous medical men of the day, to attend him; and under his care Kean became sufficiently well to enable him to act on the Saturday following that of his first performance of Richard III. Meanwhile Cecil Street was blocked from mid-day till noon with the coaches of those anxious to learn the condition of his health; whilst messages of inquiry and congratulation were hourly received by him from friends and strangers.

On the evening when he played Richard for the second time at Drury Lane the house was crowded from floor to ceiling, and amongst the brilliant audience sat Lord Byron, then in the twenty-sixth year of his age, and in the bright dawn of that fame soon to rise to its dazzling meridian. Endowed with physical beauty most rare in man, gifted with a genius of magnificent promise, fated with a temperament little understood by his kind, a halo of romance and flavour of mystery surrounded him which lent singular attraction to his name. Already had he published his *Hours of Idleness*, satirized his critics in stanzas over which mankind still smiles, taken his seat in the House of Lords, travelled in the East, swam from Sestos to Abydos, loved the Maid of Athens, given to the world some cantos of *Childe Harold*, and having returned to England, became the observed of all observers.

He had been absent from town for some weeks, and therefore had not seen Kean act, but hearing much of the tragedian, now hastened to be present. Readily swayed by all that was finest in nature and art, and easily roused to enthusiastic admiration, Byron beheld Kean's representation with wonder and delight, and henceforth the new actor had no more ardent partisan than the poet. His impressions are best conveyed in the words which, soon after leaving the theatre that night, he wrote in his diary—"Just returned from seeing Kean in Richard. By Jove! he is a soul. Life, nature, truth, without exaggeration or diminution. Richard is a man, and Kean is Richard."

The poet's admiration was unchecked by the fact of the tragedian's cold, traces of which were readily perceptible. But though it interfered with the sweetness of his voice, he was listened to with the uttermost attention, and rewarded with the heartiest applause; and when at the end of the play it was announced he would repeat his performance on Monday, the audience, believing the committee enforced his appearance, received the statement with violent disapprobation. Cries of " Shame ! shame ! " and " No ! no ! " accompanied by hisses, rang through the house. The *Times* of Monday trusted the managers would not think of " doing him, and eventually themselves, so great an injury," as to bring him forward again till his recovery was completed, or at least much further advanced. " One feels quite sorry," adds this journal, " to find him straining himself as he is compelled to do."   His health had become not only a subject of interest, but a matter of importance to the public ; and on the surmise gaining ground that he was being forced to play more frequently than was good for his condition, the managers sought to free themselves from an imputation of injustice. Therefore Arnold begged Kean would allow him to contradict the report.   Accordingly the tragedian wrote him the following letter, which appeared in the papers—

"DEAR SIR,

"I have great pleasure in authorizing you to contradict, in the most unequivocal terms, the report to which you allude. You have never pressed me to appear on the stage one day earlier than was perfectly agreeable to my own feelings, and you are aware that I have wanted no other spur to exertion than the gratification of appearing before a public who have conferred on my humble efforts the distinction of so much flattering applause. I am happy to say I am in perfect health, and at the service of the theatre whenever and as often as you think proper to call on me.

> "I am, dear sir,
>
> > "Yours sincerely,
> >
> > > "EDMUND KEAN."

His performances were therefore continued, and future prospects being now bright with promise, Nance Carey once more appeared upon the scene to claim the assistance of her son; not now her only child, for she had, whilst Edmund Kean struggled in the provinces, given birth to two children—a girl named Phœbe Carey, and a boy called Henry Darnley, both of whom eventually became players. Edmund Kean allowed her a pension of fifty pounds a year from this time until the year of his death.

CHAPTER V.

WHEN Edmund Kean arrived in London in the month of November, 1813, John Philip Kemble was regarded as the greatest actor on the English stage. A native of Preston in Lancashire, he was born in the year 1757. Kemble was therefore Kean's senior by thirty years. His father, Roger Kemble, had in his day been well known as the manager of a strolling company which periodically visited the northern counties, and was held in fair repute by the rustics whose patronage he sought.

In the tenth year of his age John Kemble made his first appearance on the stage. His father's company of comedians, whilst at the famous town of Worcester, performed "a celebrated historical play" called *Charles the First*, the *dramatis personæ* of which, as it was announced, would be "dressed in ancient habits according to the fashion of those times." On this occasion James Duke of York was represented by Master John Kemble, the Duke of Richmond by Mr. Siddons, and the Princess Elizabeth by Sarah Kemble, who afterwards became his wife. This child, who twelve years previously had been born in a low public-house called the Shoulder of Mutton, in High Street, Brecknock, was destined to become England's greatest tragic actress.

Now Roger Kemble being well-to-do, decided that his eldest son, John Philip, should become a priest, for the family were Roman Catholics, and had given to the Church at least one member, who had been martyred in days of persecution. The lad was therefore sent to a seminary at Sedley Park in Staffordshire, and subsequently to the university of Douay in France, where he was chiefly remarkable amongst his fellows for his powers of declamation. Returning to England at the age of eighteen, he declared his intention of becoming a player, much to the regret of his father, who, in order that his son might have personal experience of the hardships of an actor's life, and therefore see the errors of his way, refused him a place in his company; and sent him forth to battle with the world unaided.

Whilst he had been at Douay his sister Sally had played a leading part in a romantic comedy in real life. Siddons, who for some years had been a member of her father's troop, a versatile actor and a comely fellow, fell in love with her, and finding favour in her eyes, desired to marry her. This wish met with opposition from her parents; their daughter, being but in her sixteenth year, was considered over young to marry yet, and he, who depended on his salary for subsistence, was not such a husband as they would choose for her. Therefore, to remove her from her lover, whom they trusted she would speedily forget, they placed her in a situation as maid and companion to Lady Mary Great-head, of Guy's Cliff, in Warwickshire. This position was uncongenial to Sarah Kemble, parting her as it did from the calling in which she delighted, and from the man whom she loved; but she endured it for upwards of two years, towards the end of which time her constancy to Siddons gained her parents' consent to her marriage.

The young couple then joined a company of players whose varying successes they shared, until, being at Cheltenham, Mrs. Siddons attracted the attention of my Lord and Lady Bruce, afterwards Earl and Countess of

Aylesbury, who were drinking the waters at this fashionable resort. My lord was a man of influence, a patron of the arts, an admirer of genius, and possessing a critical faculty, saw and acknowledged Mrs. Siddons' powers. Therefore, on returning to town he commended her to David Garrick, and requested he would engage her for his theatre. Garrick, then in the last months of his management at Drury Lane, commissioned a friend to attend her performances, and give his opinion of her merits; and eventually, on the strength of this critic's praise, she was engaged for Drury Lane Theatre.

It seemed to her the goal was now won, and that she at the age of twenty had reached a position which most members of the calling she followed had failed to attain. Her hopes were short-lived. Her first appearance before a London audience was made on the 29th of December, 1775, in the character of Portia, but attracted little attention. A second chance of playing an important part was not given her for some time, for Mrs. Yates, Mrs. Abington, and Miss Young reigned queens of the Drury Lane stage, and it was indeed perilous to the manager's peace and health to introduce a rival to their high claims. Presently Mrs. Siddons was cast for a part in a farce called *Love's Metamorphoses*, than which nothing more unsuited to her talents could be found. But Garrick, now giving his series of farewell performances, having some perception of the merit underlying the quiet surface of this young actress's manner, cast her for the character of Mrs. Strickland in the *Suspicious Husband*, he playing Ranger; and subsequently she acted Lady Anne to his Richard III. But her performances gave little promise of the wondrous powers that were a few years later to rouse the public to the highest pitch of enthusiasm, and at the close of the season she was not re-engaged for Drury Lane. She therefore returned to the provinces in 1776, and played at Birmingham.

It was at this time her brother John Kemble began life as a player; and aware that she was held in fair esteem at this theatre, he offered his services to its manager, but no vacancy could be found for him. Mrs. Siddons, who was ever remarkable for the interest she took in the fortunes of her family, recommended him to a manager named Chamberlain, then at Wolverhampton, whose company he joined. Then began his experiences of the brief triumphs and certain disappointments of a stroller's life; hard work taught him many a useful lesson; privations begot gratitude for small mercies. The means he used to gain popularity were many; occasionally he recited odes between the acts, read scenes from Shakespeare, and whilst at Cheltenham introduced a novel entertainment in two parts, the first consisting of a lecture upon eloquence by himself, the second of conjuring tricks by an actor named Carlton. Times indeed were hard upon him now and then; and it is recorded that being on one occasion locked in his bedroom, a prisoner for debt due to a landlady whose husband lay ill in the chamber beneath Kemble's temporary prison, he conceived the idea of spinning a top on the floor, until the good woman thought well of sacrificing her rent to her peace, and bade him depart.

Meanwhile Mrs. Siddons was working hard, playing comedy and tragedy by night, washing and ironing her husband's and her children's clothes by day; keeping cheerful withal, having no vindictive feeling for the verdict of London playgoers, but bearing her fate with cheerfulness. The following year, 1777, room was found in the company for John Kemble, and he joined his sister; but how strange is it, in the light of modern times, to narrate, that on their return visit to Birmingham the poor players " were informed against " as rogues and vagabonds, and obliged by their worships the magistrates to get them gone with good speed. Their luck in Liverpool was scarce better; but an account of what there befell them is best related in a letter heretofore not printed, written by John Kemble to Mrs. Inchbald the dramatist. "Our affairs here are dreadful," he writes. "On Monday night we opened our theatre. Before the play began Mr. Younger advanced before the curtain, if possible to prevent any riot with which he had publicly been threatened for presuming to bring any company to Liverpool who had not played before the king. In vain did he attempt to oratorize, the remorseless villains threw up their hats, hissed, kicked, stamped, bawled, did everything to prevent his being heard. After two or three fruitless entreaties, and being saluted with volleys of potatoes and broken bottles, he thought proper to depute Siddons as his advocate, who entered bearing a board large enough to secure his person, inscribed with Mr. Younger's petition to be heard. The rogues would hear nothing, and Siddons may thank his wooden protector that his bones are whole. Mrs. Siddons entered next P. S., and Mrs. Knieveton O. P., *mais ausi infortunce.* Mrs. Knieveton had the misfortune to tumble down in convulsions on the boards; the wretches laughed, and would willingly have sent a peal of shouts after her into the next world loud enough to have burst the gates of destruction. They next extinguished all the lights round the house, then jumped upon the stage, brushed every lamp out with their hats, took back their money, left the theatre, and determined themselves to repeat this till they had another company. Well, madam, I was going to ask you what you think of all this, but I can see you laughing. I had almost forgot to tell you every wall in the city is covered with verse and prose expressive of the contempt they hold us in."

Having spent about two years in this company, John Kemble applied for and obtained an engagement from the famous Tate Wilkinson, manager of the York circuit. Kemble had now more opportunity for the display of his increasing talents. One night during the month of October, 1778, he played Macbeth at Hull with such success, that henceforth he was entrusted with leading parts. He was now anxious to represent a character suitable to his own powers, and therefore wrote a tragedy called *Belisarius*, full of long speeches and dreadful deeds, the whole plentifully besmeared with blood, which was put on the boards for a single night. He subsequently sent the play to Harris of Covent Garden, but it was returned to him unopened, as Kemble declared, with the usual expression of regret that it was unsuitable to his stage.

This grieved its author sorely, as such disappointments will in youth, and he wrote despairingly to his friend Mrs. Inchbald, " My health declines every day. I have neither spirits, in which I never abounded, nor genius, of which inclination perhaps wholly supplied the place, to attempt anything for my improvement in polite letters. You know me, I believe, well enough to feel for me when I say, that with all my ambition I am afraid I shall live and die a common fellow."

Such fears as this, expressed in a moment of despondency, were futile, for he was destined to rise in the estimation of men. Having played with success at Hull, York, and Leeds for a couple of seasons, he, on being offered an engagement in Ireland, crossed the Channel to act in the Smock Alley theatre, at what was then considered an excellent salary of five pounds a week. Here his Hamlet, Macbeth, Richard III., and Alexander the Great were lauded. His elocution was distinct if monotonous, his manner dignified if formal, his appearance picturesque though inanimate. Whilst he played in Ireland, Mrs. Siddons had been acting at Bath to audiences described as " the most elegant in Great Britain," and her fame reaching the capital, offers of an engagement were made her by the managers of Drury Lane Theatre, and accepted by her. Accordingly she appeared in that house on the 20th of October, 1782, seven years later than the date on which she had first played on that stage.

Her performance created the wildest sensation amongst all lovers of the drama; in a single night her fame was established, henceforth she was recognized as the queen of tragedy. Hazlitt narrates, that the enthusiasm she excited " had something idolatrous about it; she was regarded less with admiration than wonder, as if a being of a superior order had dropped from another sphere to awe the world with the majesty of her appearance. She raised tragedy to the skies or brought it down from thence. It was something above nature. We can conceive of nothing grander. She embodied to our imagination the fables of mythology, or the heroic and deified mortals of elder time. She was not less than a goddess, or than a prophetess inspired by the gods. Power was seated on her brow, passion emanated from her breast as from a shrine. She was Tragedy personified. She was the stateliest ornament of the public mind. She was not only the idol of the people, she not only hushed the tumultuous shouts of the pit in breathless expect-ation, and quenched the blaze of surrounding beauty in silent tears, but to the retired and lonely student through long years of solitude her face has shone as if an eye had appeared from heaven; her name has been as if a voice had opened the chambers of the human heart, or as if a trumpet had awakened the sleeping and the dead. To have seen Mrs. Siddons was an event in every one's life."

She now experienced the pleasures and penalties of fame: crowds followed her through the streets; the drawing-rooms of the great were thrown open to her, and when she appeared there, guests mounted upon chairs and sofas to observe her movements; statesmen sought conversation with her, and her merest remarks were listened to with bated breath. But in the midst of this enthusiasm she remained calm and dignified. "Why, this is a leaden goddess we are all worshipping," quoth lively Mrs. Thrale, "but we will soon gild her." To cover her with the tarnished metal of conventional mannerism was not, however, within the power of this vivacious dame. But bearing in mind her grandeur and sublimity, it is hard to reconcile her brother's idea of her being "one of the best comic singers of the day." Certain it is that before she attained greatness she had, in order to attract country audiences, to appear not only in farce, but in ballad operas, and sing blithesome songs; and assuredly she did all things well upon the stage.

At the close of the season the members of the Bar presented her with a hundred guineas, "as an acknowledgment of the pleasure and instruction her talents had given them." She then went to Edinburgh, where she received a thousand pounds for ten nights' performance, together with several presents. Later on she visited Ireland, where the enthusiasm she created if anything exceeded that she already caused in London.

Whilst she was here negotiations were made for the engagement of John Kemble as a member of the Drury Lane company; and accordingly he made his appearance as Hamlet at the national theatre on the 30th of September, 1783. The relationship he bore to the great actress, then the theme of every tongue, drew a crowded audience to witness his first performance. He was received with applause, and a long period of prosperity set in for him.

His face was well cut and handsome, his figure tall and portly, his presence graceful and commanding, and seeing him night after night as the representation of noble heroes, a daughter of Lord North fell violently in love with him, a fact she made manifest in letters she addressed to him. Her father, becoming aware of her infatuation, remonstrated with her, but in vain ; and his subsequent threats were answered by the avowal that John Kemble was the only one she would ever wed. Lord North being a shrewd man, believed he could avert an event he dreaded as a calamity. Therefore he waited on Kemble, plainly stated that if he married his daughter she should never receive a penny from him, but if within a fortnight he wed any other lady, he, Lord North, would give him four thousand pounds in return for his compliance. Kemble, who valued money greatly, accepted his offer, proposed to and was accepted as her husband by Mrs. Brierton, an actress, and speedily married.

And having fulfilled Lord North's desire, he waited upon him for his reward; but his lordship, being wily, professed total forgetfulness of his bargain. He coldly inquired on what ground Mr. Kemble imagined he had any interest in his domestic concerns, and ended by stating, that although, in common with all men of taste, he admired him as an actor, yet he wished his perform-ances confined to the theatre. Kemble left his presence a sadder man. The story, which by no means reflected credit on Lord North, was not kept secret by him, and the kind friends, ever ready to ridicule a successful man, made merry over the tale, which was widely repeated, and at length found place in Oxberry's biography of Kemble.

In 1788, whilst Edmund Kean was an infant of twelve months, John Kemble became stage manager of Drury Lane Theatre, where he laboured zealously for the advancement of dramatic art by restoring the original text of Shakespeare's plays, and insisting on proper regard being paid to accuracy of costume and architecture. Three years later he resigned this office, that he might travel through France and Spain. Having spent about two years abroad, he returned to England, and purchased a sixth share in Covent Garden Theatre, of which he became part manager. Mrs. Siddons had up to this time played at Drury Lane, but on her brother becoming part proprietor of the rival house she joined its forces, and now in the fulness of her fame drew crowded audiences in her track. Custom had not staled her infinite variety. "In bursts of indignation or grief," we are told, "in apostrophes and inarticulate sounds, she raised the soul of passion to its height or sunk it in despair."

Her acting had long ago attracted the admiration even of Queen Charlotte, whose knowledge of the language spoken by her subjects was limited, and Her Majesty was wont to command Mrs. Siddons and John Kemble to read in her royal presence. Fanny Burney, who was dresser to the queen, on one occasion received the great actress when she was commanded to appear at Windsor, and describes her as " the queen of tragedy, sublime, elevated, and solemn. In face and person truly noble and commanding; in manners quiet and stiff; in voice deep and dragging; and in conversation formal, sententious, calm, and dry. I expected her to have been all that is interesting; the delicacy and sweetness with which she seizes every opportunity to strike and to captivate upon the stage had persuaded me that her mind was formed with that peculiar susceptibility which in different modes must give equal powers to attract and to delight in commom life. But I was very much mistaken. As a stranger, I must have admired her noble appearance and beautiful countenance, and have regretted that nothing in her conversation kept pace with their promise; and as a celebrated actress I had still only to do the same."

The honour of reading in the presence of royalty was the sole reward she received for her labours so long as they continued, for their Majesties were notable for an economy which has been called by harsh names. Nor were her duties rendered lighter by kindness, the lack of which eventually ended them; for one day when

Mrs. Siddons, then soon to become a mother, had been standing some two hours, it being forbidden by court etiquette to sit in the presence of Majesty, she fainted, and would have fallen, but that John Kemble rushed forward and caught her, whereon the queen, grasping her snuff-box, hastily rose, and, followed by the princesses, quitted the apartment, "that the actress might sit down." To the credit of John Kemble and Mrs. Siddons be it stated, that henceforth when commanded to appear before royalty they invariably found themselves suddenly indisposed.

In 1812, two years before Kean's appearance at Drury Lane, Mrs. Siddons took leave of the stage, and her retirement was followed by the sincere regret of the public. At the close of the same season John Kemble withdrew from Covent Garden for the purpose of making a prolonged tour through the provinces. He returned, however, on the 11th of January, 1814, just fifteen days previous to the night on which Kean first played Shylock at Drury Lane. All it was possible to acquire by severe study, careful methods, and active intelligence were Kemble's; but he needed that subtle power called genius, for lack of which nought else can compensate. He had long enjoyed popularity, but already a player was at hand who was destined to fling him from the pedestal he had occupied for many years. Mrs. Siddons had certainly prepared his way with the public, and but for her it is certain he would never have attained the position as England's greatest actor, for the genius she undoubtedly possessed flung its glory upon him.

He had re-introduced to the stage the cold, passionless style of acting which Garrick had banished, and which Kean was destined to drive again from the boards. His elocution, when not marred by asthma, was faultless in its pronunciation, but measured, hard, and monotonous; his face, finely moulded and massive, lacked animation and expression; his gestures, graceful and appropriate, were carefully studied and mechanical. John Howard Payne the dramatist said, " He enlarged his legs and arms by pads, and consulted pictures and artists to produce personal effects"; whilst Mrs. Siddons complained, "My brother John in his most impetuous outbursts is always careful to avoid any discomposure of his dress or deportment, but in the whirlpool of passion I lose all thought of such matters "; and Haydon the painter added, " Kemble came into a part with a stately dignity, as if he disdained to listen to nature, however she might whisper, until he had examined and weighed the value of her counsel."

Assuredly he lacked the great and necessary art of concealing art. Grand and impressive he could be in such parts as Cato, Coriolanus, and Brutus, but from beginning to end of his performances no touch of nature was present, and the heroes he represented were respected but not loved. There lay the perceptible blemish. In the earlier part of his career he had striven to play comedy, in which, Jack Bannister used to say, "he was as merry as a funeral and as light as an elephant." However, he desired to prove he was all he believed himself to be; and was anxious the press should share in the opinions he held of his own acting. Therefore when he was about to act the part of Charles Surface, he wrote to Major Topham, who was not only a biographer and dramatist, but the proprietor and conductor of a journal called *The World*, informing him he had placed three of his friends on the free list of the theatre, and hoping "he would have the goodness to give orders to his people to speak favourably of Charles, as more depends on that than he could possibly be aware of." Not satisfied with this, Kemble also wrote to Mrs. Wells, an eccentric woman and "a bold player," whose influence over Major Topham was notorious, requesting she would ask the Major to commend his performance in *The World*. And she, complying, received the following from Topham, which, together with Kemble's note, she published in her memoirs—"I received your letter where you mention Kemble's wish to be puffed. You may inform Mr. Este (the editor) from me, I will not sacrifice the credit of my paper for all the admissions in Europe, to puff either the Siddons or the Kembles in comedy."

In the course of time, and with the aid of public opinion, John Kemble came to the conclusion his cold and stately manner was unsuited to comedy, and therefore abandoned it wholly. A flattering host with whom he was dining one day, regretted this resolve, for he considered Charles Surface had been lost to the stage since the days of Gentleman Smith, and added, that Kemble's representation should have been considered as Charles's restoration; whereon another guest whispered, it should rather be termed Charles's martyrdom. Kemble heard this witty remark, and received it with good humour; nay, he even ventured to tell a story against himself concerning the playing of the part.

"Well, now," he said, "that gentleman is not altogether singular in his opinion, as, if you will give me leave, I will prove to you. A few months ago, having unfortunately taken what is usually called a glass too much, on my return, late at night, I inadvertently quarrelled with a gentleman in the street. This gentleman very properly called on me next morning for an explanation of what was certainly more accidental than intentional. 'Sir,' said I, 'when I commit an error I am always ready to atone for it; and if you will only name any reasonable reparation in my power, I——' 'Sir,' interrupted the gentleman, 'at once I meet your proposal, and name one. Solemnly promise, in the presence of this my friend, that you will never play Charles Surface again, and I am perfectly satisfied.' Well, I did promise," continued Kemble, "not from nervousness, as you may suppose, gentlemen, but because, though Sheridan was pleased to say that he liked me in the part, I certainly did not like myself in it, no more than that gentleman who has just done me the favour to call it Charles's martyrdom."

Another worthy critic, it must be remembered, commended John Kemble's playing of the part; Charles Lamb considered "the weighty sense of Kemble made up for more personal incapacity than he had to answer for. His harshest tones in this part came steeped and dulcified in good-humour. He made his defects a grace. His exact declamatory manner, as he managed it, only served to convey the points of his dialogue with more precision. It seemed to head the shafts to carry them deeper." But all the while, it must be remembered, Charles Lamb had never seen Gentleman Smith represent Charles Surface.

The opinion John Kemble held of himself was one most gratifying to his vanity. Frederick Reynolds narrates, that on one occasion at a dinner, when the tragedian had drank deeply, after the fashion of the day, and boasted freely of his great abilities and wondrous success, a merry neighbour whispered audibly, "I would go barefooted to Holyhead and back only to see a fellow one half so clever as he thinks himself."

His manner was cold and reserved with his associates at the theatre, and he was therefore generally unpopular with them. Because of his complexion, they usually called him Black Jack; and by this term he was invariably spoken of by George Frederick Cooke, a really fine actor, whose brief and reckless career ended before Kean's advent in London. Between Cooke and Kemble no love existed, for Cooke openly derided Kemble's pompous acting, and Kemble plainly despised Cooke for his dissipated habits. When drunk, as was too frequently the case, poor Cooke was wont to complain that "with the voice of an emasculated French horn, and the face of an itinerant Israelite, Black Jack would compete with me, sir—with me, George

Frederick Cooke; wanted me to play Horatio to his Hamlet, sir. Let him play Sir Pertinax, sir (a favourite character of Cooke's), that's all. I should like to hear him attempt the accent!" When Cooke went to America some idea of his approaching fate possibly crossed his mind, for he said he "didn't want to die in this country; John Kemble would laugh." But Cooke returned to England never again; and if Kemble did not mourn the unfortunate actor's untimely end, he certainly profited by it, for Cooke was the only player at that time greatly his superior, there being no other tragedian worthy of the name upon the stage.

For years John Kemble had suffered from asthma, so that it became painful to hear him gasp and cough during his performances. One night when, as Macbeth, he lay dead upon the stage, he felt almost suffocated, and at length was obliged to sit up and cough, to the great amusement of the house; hearing of which, witty Jack Bannister said, "Ah, poor fellow, it must have been a churchyard cough."

John Kemble, being the best tragic actor the stage had up to this time possessed, was admired and lauded by a large section of playgoers; but now the force and fervour, earnestness and passion of the Drury Lane tragedian brought his cold and pompous, stiff and ponderous manner into sharp contrast; a new light was cast upon his playing, revealing an unlikeness to nature before scarce heeded. But the force of habit is strong within all men, and those who had long given him their full allegiance were loath to turn from him in favour of a competitor.

And now could comparisons between them be more fitly made, for Kean, it was stated, was to play Hamlet, a character Kemble had long since made his own—one in which it was considered he was seen to greatest advantage. Neither did Kean spare thought nor care in the study of this part. Years ago, whilst tramping along lonely highways, he had meditated upon the effects he might, as the Prince of Denmark, produce upon provincial audiences; but now when the most enlightened people in the kingdom crowded to witness his efforts, his whole mind was set upon achieving a signal success. Words and sentences were pronounced and spoken repeatedly in various tones, until his ear caught the most effective key; expressions and gestures were practised persistently before mirrors, until his sense of fitness was satisfied; actions that subsequently seemed the inspiration of a moment were deliberately conceived and practised; nay, he counted the very steps he was to take upon the stage before reaching a

certain spot or uttering a certain phrase. Genius he
undoubtedly possessed, but he was wise enough to know
labour was necessary to its perfection.

The announcement of his performance caused
general excitement, and on the evening of Saturday
the 12th of March, 1814, the struggle at the doors of
Drury Lane Theatre hours before the play began
threatened to prove disastrous.   Not merely women,
but men, overcome by heat and long fasting, fainted;
cries for help rose from those who, no longer able to
endure, sought escape from the dense, closely-packed
mass of humanity by which they were surrounded.
Shortly after the doors opened the theatre was filled
to the utmost limits, from floor to ceiling. Then arose
a din from a multitude of voices as friend shouted to
friend, or details were recounted of the fight for place,
and inquiries made for the articles of dress lost in the
fray.   Amidst this continued confusion the music of
the orchestra was inaudible, nay, even when the curtain
rose on the first scene the excitement was unsubdued,
and the voice of the ghost was unheard in the house.
But presently, as the royal court of Denmark assembled, silence fell upon all. Then entered Hamlet,
slow-paced, his air full of grief, his countenance expressive of sorrow over-deep for words. That first

impression, on which an actor most depends, was all he could desire. Later the pathos of his tones, the languor of his gait, the deep meaning of his looks, fascinated his audience, and in his interests and concerns bound him to their hearts. One and all felt a new interpretation of a character, the most strange and subtle the master has drawn, was about to be given them. Nor were they mistaken.

His surprise on beholding his father's ghost, his confidence in following its steps, the sorrow and reverence mingling in his voice when he addressed it, were full of poetry and power. In the scene where he broke from his friends to follow this distressed shade, he kept his sword pointing behind him to prevent them following him, instead of holding it before him to protect himself from the spirit, as had formerly been done. The manner of his taking Guildenstern and Rosencrantz underneath each arm with pretence of communicating his secret, whilst really trifling with them, produced a fine effect; so likewise did his acting in the closet scene with his mother. Here, as the *Examiner* remarked, " his tones, as usual, told that his heart, not his memory, was speaking; but he did not display any of the theatrical tricks which the audience had been used to expect. He did not shake his mother out of her chair, nor wave his handkerchief with a dignified whirl, nor spread his arms like a heron crucified on a barn door."

His scene with Ophelia was most full of passion and pathos; especially did it stir the house when, after commanding her to go to a nunnery, he hurried from her presence, and then, as if overcome by tenderness and regret, hastened back, and taking her right hand, kissed it fervidly. This action, Hazlitt relates, had an electric effect upon the house. "It was the finest commentary that was ever made on Shakespeare. It explained the character at once (as he meant it), as one of disappointed hope, of bitter regret, of affection suspended, not obliterated by the distractions of the scene around him." An anonymous correspondent writing to the *Examiner* says, "Two simple actions, occupying as many minutes, those noble illustrations of Shakespeare's writings,—the dying scene in *Richard the Third*, and the parting with Ophelia—are worth all the notes critical and historical, emendatory and commendatory, declamatory and defamatory, that were ever written."

The whole performance was full of beauty, originality, and poetry, which his audience recognized and applauded warmly. Again and again during the play he was greeted with ringing cheers; and for some moments after the fall of the curtain the house was in a state of wild enthusiasm. The criticisms of his acting, with the exception of that of the *Times*, were laudatory; but the dramatic censor of that journal had never been satisfied with the new actor, nor was he now. He first displayed his lack of knowledge by complaining that Kean, "who was far from well-dressed," actually came to the court without ornament or insignia, being ignorant that the Danish Order of the Elephant was not instituted until about the year 1448, whilst Hamlet is supposed to have lived before the Norman Conquest, at the time when England was connected with Denmark. This ornament John Kemble had always worn in personating the prince, and the writer doubtless considered that it was an error not to follow his example. But more remained to be said. Mr. Kean was clearly "a person of excellent good sense, and of a powerful discrimination," but he had certainly pronounced contumely in four syllables. . His figure and gait were not sufficiently graceful and dignified, he "fell off" in the last two acts; but great allowance should be made for his youth, doubtless he would im-prove. Reading such comments one is forcibly struck by a remark made in the *Examiner*, that Kean's style in Hamlet, "was too good for the public, whose taste has been vitiated by the long-established affectations of the school of Kemble." The Ophelia of this occasion was highly commended—Miss Smith, a lady of Hibernian extraction, whose real name was O'Shaughnessy. Endowed with a beautiful and expressive face, a clear and melodious voice, a well-formed and graceful figure, she had readily become a favourite with the town. Her style and manner were said closely to resemble those of Mrs. Siddons, whose merits no other actress had up to this time so nearly approached; and in her performances Kean found valuable support.

Again and again *Hamlet* was repeated to audiences whose enthusiasm remained unabated. Joe Cowen, at this time playing at Woolwich, in a company of which Robert Keeley was likewise a member, had not yet seen Kean; but being anxious to witness the performance of one concerning whom he heard much, he and Keeley walked to town one day, "and at about four o'clock in the afternoon," he writes, " we joined a crowd already assembled at the pit entrance of Drury Lane Theatre, which continued to increase by thousands before the doors were opened. Half crushed to death," he continues, for his experience were better narrated in his own words, " we found ourselves, after a desperate effort, at the back of the passage which surrounds the pit, from whence I could, by straining to my utmost height, catch a glimpse of the corner of the green curtain nearest to the top, but little Bob hadn't even that satisfaction. There, at any rate, we could not see Kean, nor live to see anything else at the end of a few hours' squeeze such as we were then enduring, and we agreed to pay the extra three-and-sixpence and go into the boxes; but as to obtaining a pass check, it was impossible. We had nearly as much trouble to get out as we had to get in, and were content to lose our three-and-sixpence apiece, and pay fourteen shillings more for the privilege of standing on a back seat of the upper tier of boxes at the corner next the stage, an excellent point of sight for a perspective view of the crown of a man's hat, or a bald spot on the head of a lady who, seated in the pit, had been obliged to take off her bonnet whether she liked it or not.

"Bruised in body, and sorely afflicted in spirit and pocket, we were just in the mood not to be easily pleased with anything or anybody. When Kean came on I was astonished. I was prepared to see a small man; but, diminished by the unusual distance and his black dress, and a mental comparison with Kemble's princely person, he appeared a perfect pigmy; his voice, unlike any I had ever heard before, perhaps from its very strangeness, was most objectionable, and I turned to Keeley, and at once pronounced him *a most decided humbug;* and if I could have got out then, I should have said so to everybody, because I honestly thought so; and if afterwards I had been convinced of his enormous genius, I might, like Taylor, the oculist and editor of the *Sun* newspaper, have persisted in my denunciation, rather than confess my incapacity at the first glance to comprehend the sublimity of Shakespeare and Nature being upon such familiar terms. But I was obliged to remain, and compelled to be silent; so invoking patience, and placing my hand on a young lady's shoulder for support, I quietly gazed on through three tedious scenes—for all the actors seemed worse than usual—till it came to the dialogue with the ghost, and at the line

'I'll call thee Hamlet—king—father,'

I was converted. I resigned the support of the lady, and employed both hands in paying the usual tribute to godlike talent. Father is not a pretty word to look at, but it is beautiful to hear when lisped by little children, or spoken by Edmund Kean in *Hamlet.*"

Whenever Kean played the theatre was crowded to excess, and the treasury received sums averaging six hundred pounds on the nights of his performances. This continued, notwithstanding the attractions held forth by the rival house; for not only did John Kemble play Brutus in *Julius Cæsar*, Wolsey in *Henry VIII.*, Coriolanus, Hamlet, and Cato, characters in which of yore his "proud peculiarity, melancholy composure, and magnificent deportment" had been lauded; but Mrs. Jordan, now at Covent Garden, was giving what were destined to be her last performances before being driven penniless and friendless into exile, through the conduct of the Duke of Clarence. And here, likewise, was Charles Young, a player belonging to the Kemble school, who a few weeks after Kean's first appearance as Richard III. sought to show the town how the wicked king might be represented with the propriety and gentility of a marionette, and so afford the public an opportunity of exercising its judgment before pledging itself an adherent of the new actor.

Charles Mayne Young, as already narrated, was the son of a famous London physician. Being born in 1777, he was ten years older than Kean. Twelve months of his early life had been spent at the Court of Denmark, where his uncle was physician, and for three years was he an Eton boy. His home life was far from happy, owing to the behaviour of his father, who was not only

a .profligate husband, but a tyrannical parent. So in-
famous was his conduct, that his wife and three sons
were obliged to quit his roof, though possessing neither
the means of support nor the certainty of shelter at the
time. A kindly relative succoured the mother and
her lads, one of whom became a surgeon, one a clerk
in the East Indian Service, and one a player. This
latter was Charles, who began life in a city office; but
becoming fascinated by the stage, desired to be an
actor. Therefore, without leaving his situation, the
salary of which helped to support his mother, he joined
an amateur theatrical club, and there, after the fashion
of many others, learned the rudiments of an art in
which he desired to excel.

At the age of one-and-twenty he made his first
appearance at Liverpool, and such progress did he
achieve, that the following year he was engaged to
play lead at Manchester. After spending an ap-
prenticeship in the provinces, he appeared at the
Haymarket in the character of Hamlet. He was
greeted kindly and applauded heartily, but in the
midst of this encouragement his quick ear detected
a solitary hiss, and turning his eyes towards the direction. whence it came, he saw the malignant face of
his father.

His acting was cold, declamatory, and dignified, knowing nothing of nature and little of passion. He acknowledged himself "a devout disciple of the Kemble school," and a portion of the public regarded him as a servile imitator. The resemblance of his style to John Kemble's was so striking, his tone and emphasis so similar, that when both actors were on the stage at the same time, it was difficult for the audience to discover which had spoken. His voice was sonorous, his attitudes graceful, his gestures proper; he pleased, but never excited; he charmed the fancy, but never touched the heart; he plunged a dagger in his breast with the same elegance, precision, and lack of emotion as he handed a chair to a lady. He had never been moved by a breath of passion, and never rose to originality; his head, not his heart, was his guide. It was said that in committing new parts to memory, he recited his speeches to a pianoforte accompaniment, by which he learned to modulate his tones; and no doubt this practice helped to give the impression of art rather than the touch of nature to his delivery. Six years before Kean flashed upon the town Charles Young had been engaged for the Covent Garden company, and from that time his life had passed uneventfully.

He indeed was wholly powerless to stem the current of popularity which had now set in Kean's favour. John Kemble had at first heard of the young actor's attraction with the calm indifference of assured superiority, believed this departure from allegiance due to him was but a momentary freak, a passing eccentricity on the part of public judgment, such as · had once hailed Master Betty as a wonder, and subsequently ignored him as a failure. But the criticisms which continually reached him from reliable sources, together with the increasing admiration of the town, caused him to seriously believe a rival had verily entered the field. Accordingly he became anxious to see Kean, and one evening, from behind the curtains of a box at Drury Lane, watched him with eagerness and surprise as he played Richard III. Leaving the house impressed by the grandeur and force of the death scene, Kemble was accosted by a friend, who asked him what he thought of the new actor. "I did not see Mr. Kean at all," he replied, "I only saw Richard." And speaking presently to James Boaden of the new favourite, he said, "Our styles of acting are so totally different, that you must not expect me to like Mr. Kean; but one thing I must say in his favour—he is at all times terribly in earnest."

Mrs. Siddons was also eager to see Kean, whom she remembered having acted with years ago in Belfast, and returning from witnessing one of his performances remarked, " His eyes are marvellous, having a sort of fascination, like that attributed to the snake." Another woman, who had enjoyed some fame in her day, was more enthusiastic concerning Kean than the retired queen of tragedy. This was Mrs. David Garrick, who had passed her eightieth year, and was now a hale, sprightly little old lady, whose dark eyes, silver hair, and calm expression gave a beauty to her age her youth had never known. An artiste, a foreigner, the widow of a great actor, her interest in all things theatrical was yet vigorous, and her chief delight consisted in visits to the playhouses. On the night of Kean's first appearance as Hamlet she had occupied her box at Drury Lane Theatre; and on his entrance, his size and appearance at once riveted her attention; then the light and expression of his eyes as he turned them on the king, and the sound of his voice as he spoke the soliloquy, completed the charm he exercised over her. That evening she who was usually garrulous remained silent and abstracted; thoughts of the past abided with her in the present, and the tears she quietly shed were alike a tribute to the powers of the living and to the memory of the dead.

Some days later she wrote a note to Thomas Dibdin, asking him to come and see her relative to a sum of money she wished to give a musician in distress. On calling at her residence in the Adelphi, Dibdin was shown into the library, a long narrow room, whose walls were lined with books. As he entered, Mrs. Garrick, dressed in black, came tripping from the far end of the apartment with all the lightness and grace of a girl of eighteen, and greeted her visitor. Having asked him to undertake the commission relative to her charity, she continued, in a voice still retaining some traces of foreign accent—

"Mr. Dipdin, I look upon you as a twick of the old school; your father was a great friend of my husband's, and I am glad you are in Drury Lane. I go now and then to my box there, and am much pleased with your new actor, Mr. Kean."

Dibdin assured her he would be proud to learn her opinion.

"But Mr. Kean," she continued, "is like Mr. Garrick himself. Mr. Kean could never have seen Mr. Garrick, who was dead before your new actor was born; yet he not only speaks some speeches in the style of that *good* actor" (marking the adjective with impressive accents, and looking reverentially at the picture of Garrick over the fireplace), " but he seems to me to choose the very same board to speak them on ; and this, Mr. Dipdin, is no small compliment when the worth of my husband is still twinkling in my ears."

This led to an introduction of Kean, whom Mrs. Garrick received with a mixture of the courtesy becoming a hostess and the patronage pardonable in age. Taking him by one hand she led him to a chair, leather-seated and high-backed,—" it was my husband's favourite," she explained,—and then they fell into discourse. What scenes and memories, vivid with the figures of men and women now no more, rose to the surface of her mind; voices long unheard spoke again, the dead lived; years fell from her life as sand through the fingers of a child, and she was young once more. Stories were told more strange than fiction; comments made, traditions bequeathed. She assured her visitor he was the only actor worthy of succeeding her husband; and then came comparisons, when, assuming the privilege of a critic, she praised and chided, and ended by making him rehearse the closet scene in *Hamlet*, and assured him he must in future play it with more vigour, after the manner of dear David.

Kean secured not only her admiration, but her friendship, and one day whilst he was with her she unlocked an escritoire, and took a parcel from a private drawer. This she handled with reverence, and sighed over as she untied the string. Then she showed him a pair of gloves of quaint fashion and great age, which had belonged to Shakespeare, and which she intended leaving to Mrs. Siddons; and unwrapping them from many folds of paper, she displayed the stage jewels worn by Garrick. " No one," she said, " has been found worthy of them until now. Take them—they are yours."

CHAPTER VI.

MEANWHILE Kean was carefully studying the part of Othello, the character he next meant to personate. His determination drew forth various comments, and for days discussions raged in club and coffee-houses, in drawing-room and green-room, as to whether his figure and manner were suitable to the representation of the Moor of Venice. Those who remembered Garrick narrated their impressions of his Othello, and laughingly quoted Colley Cibber's statement that he thought David was the black boy who carried Desdemona's kettle, and Kemble's partisans felt certain stage history would repeat itself. Details whispered by those who took part in or witnessed the rehearsals were eagerly sought and proudly retailed; expectation rose to a high pitch. The date of the performance was fixed for the fifth of May (1814).

Although little more than three months had elapsed since Kean first played at Drury Lane, a change had taken place in his fate and fortune, such as years could not accomplish in the lives of other men. He who had been treated with general contempt was now regarded with universal admiration; his poverty had given place to affluence, his struggles with obscurity ended in certain victory. He had said if he should succeed he must go mad, but as yet the erratic tendencies of his nature were subdued, and the world went well with him.

On the evening of the fifth of May the most famous men and women of the day gathered to see his performance of Othello. In the green-room groups of those proud to .. themselves his friends waited until opportunity allowed them to express their hopes for his success, whilst his dressing-room was crowded by more privileged admirers. And when he made his appearance, the wild tumult of applause which greeted him, the sight of the brilliant circle of fair women in the boxes, the sea of human faces in pit and gallery, might well warm the heart and string the nerves to highest tension of an actor less sensitive than he.

The highest expectations formed of him were not disappointed ; from the first act to the last his audience were dazzled by the wild glare of his brilliancy, spell-bound by the force of his power; throughout all, repeated outbursts of passion swayed them as boughs tossed in a tempest. The third act was especially remarkable as a masterpiece of exquisite conception and profound pathos. Never had the great dramatist been so interpreted before; his spirit had entered into the heart of this actor, and expressed itself by word, look, and motion. "The tone of his voice," says the *Morning Chronicle*, "when he delivered the apostrophe, 'O now for ever farewell the tranquil mind,' struck the heart and the imagination like some divine music. The look, the action, the expression of voice with which he accompanied the exclamation, 'Not a jot; not a jot,' the reflection, 'I felt not Cassio's kisses on her lips,' his vow of revenge against Cassio, and abandonment of his love for Desdemona, laid open the very tumult and agony of the soul." Hazlitt supposed his Othello the finest piece of acting in the world. "In one part," he says, "where he listens in dumb despair to the fiend-like insinuations of Iago, he presented the very face, the marble aspect of Dante's Count Ugolino. On his fixed eyelids 'horror sat plumed.' In another part, where a gleam of hope or of tenderness returns to subdue the tumult of his passion, his voice broke in faltering accents from his over-charged breast. His lips might be said less to utter words than to distil drops of blood gushing from his heart. His exclamation on seeing his wife, 'I cannot think but Desdemona's honest,' was 'the glorious triumph of exceeding love '— a thought flashing conviction on his mind, and irradiating his countenance with joy like sudden sunshine. In fact, almost every scene or sentence of this extraordinary exhibition is a masterpiece of natural passion. The convulsed motion of the hands, and the involuntary swelling of the veins in the forehead, in some of the most painful situations, should not only suggest topics of critical panegyric, but might furnish studies to the painter or the sculptor."

But all the criticisms on his acting were not so eloquent or so favourable as this; and an amusing story is recorded by the biographer of Charles Kean concerning the tragedian and Mrs. Garrick. The latter, on calling one morning in May, found him in a state of unusual excitement. He received her abruptly, and retired quickly, conduct which much astonished the old lady, who, turning to Mrs. Kean, inquired what was the matter with her husband.

"Oh," replied Mrs. Kean, "you mustn't mind him; he has just read a spiteful notice of his Othello in one of the newspapers which has terribly vexed him."

"But why should he mind that?" asked Mrs. Garrick; "he is above the papers, and can afford to be abused."

"Yes," replied Mrs. Kean, "but he says the article is well written; but for that he wouldn't care for its comments."

"Then, my dear," said Mrs. Garrick, soothingly, "he should do as David did, and he would be spared this annoyance."

"What's that?" said the anxious wife, hoping her husband might follow the great man's example.

"Write the articles himself; David always did."

But the vexation arising from this criticism was soon forgotten in a compliment paid him by Richard Brinsley Sheridan, the day of whose brilliant life was now drawing towards its night. Hearing much of Kean's Othello, he was anxious to see his performance, but would not visit Drury Lane; for, owing to some offence received from the managing committee, he had vowed never to set his foot within the theatre. By a mutual friend his desire was conveyed to Kean, with a request that the tragedian would favour him by reading some passages from the play. To this suggestion Kean assented with pleasure, and calling upon him, he found the author of the *School for Scandal*, the companion of Burke, Johnson, Goldsmith, and Reynolds, the accuser of Warren Hastings, lying on a sofa in a room sadly despoiled of its furniture by the brokers. His once bright and handsome face was sickly and sad, his figure worn by illness and dissipation. Kean read him the chief scenes from *Othello*, at which those wonderful gray eyes that had once sparkled with wit grew bright once more, and anon were dimmed with tears; for since Garrick left the stage no one had heard the divine words of this play spoken with such pathos and passion. At the conclusion Sheridan thanked the tragedian heartily—he was poor in all save thanks,—and hoped they might meet frequently in the future. But this was not to be, for two months later Richard Brinsley Sheridan lay sleeping in Westminster Abbey.

Before the surprise and excitement caused by his playing of Othello had ceased, it was announced that Kean would represent Iago. Nor had he cause to fear the comparison of his acting in this character with his

masterly representation of the Moor. The one in
every way contrasted the other, yet each possessed
almost equal merit. Iago in his hands became a gay,
light-hearted monster, a careless, cordial, comfortable
villain, ready to ruin a woman's reputation with a
merry jest, or willing to murder a friendly life with
a graceful sword-thrust. The easy familiarity and
natural tone with which he delivered the text was
delightful; the complete preservation of character, carefully conceived and excellently executed, was admirable.
A specimen of his by-play mentioned in the pages of
the *Examiner* is worth recording as an example of his
care in trifling incidents as in great scenes. He kills
Roderigo, thinking by his death to make all compact
and secure; his whole fortune hinges on the event; it
is, as he says, the thing which is to make or to mar him
quite. The actors of this part generally seemed to be
of a different opinion; they stabbed Roderigo, and then
walked away with perfect ease and satisfaction. But
Kean knew better; he repeated the atrocious thrust
till he supposed no life remained in his victim. Yet,
aware Roderigo's existence was a matter much too
serious to be left in doubt, he even, when presently
conversing with those around him, continually cast his
eyes towards the body of his victim with an intensity

that would fain convince itself of the surety of his death; nay, occasionally he walked by it seemingly with carelessness, certainly with purpose, glancing at the motionless limbs as if he expected yet feared to notice them quivering with life, his manner cool, his anxiety perceptible only by his furtive glances.

Iago was pronounced by the *Morning Chronicle* "the most faultless of his performances, the most consistent and entire; the least overdone of all his parts, though full of point, spirit, and brilliancy."

Mindful of their obligations to him, the shareholders of the theatre presented him with five hundred pounds, and four of the committee each gave him a hundred pound share in the theatre. Lord Essex made him a present of a handsome sword; Wroughton of a point lace collar Garrick had invariably worn when he played Richard III.; and Lord Byron of a gold snuff-box, having a boar hunt wrought in mosaic on the lid; and henceforth Kean adopted a boar as his crest, as had King Richard III. Long since the poet had been asked to meet Kean at a dinner to be given at Holland House; for the tragedian's company was now sought by the most distinguished men and women of the day, and my Lady Holland would fain include him in the brilliant circle, which numbered amongst others

such distinguished guests as Tom Moore, Lady Blessing-
ton, Count D'Orsay, Ugo Foscolo, Samuel Rogers, and
Sir Thomas Lawrence. On being bidden by Lady
Holland to her dinner-party, Lord Byron made the
following entry in his diary—" An invitation to dine at
Holland House to meet Kean. He is worth meeting,
and I hope, by getting into good society, he will be
prevented from falling like Cooke. He is greater now
on the stage, and off he should never be less. There
is a stupid and underrating criticism upon him in one
of the newspapers. I thought that last night, though
great, he rather underacted more than the first time.
This may be the effect of these cavils, but I hope that
he has more sense than to mind them. He cannot
expect to maintain his present eminence, or to advance
still higher, without the envy of his green-room fellows,
or the quibbling of their admirers. But if he don't
beat them all, why then—merit hath no purchase in
' these costermonger days.' "

Byron's acquaintance with Kean soon ripened into
intimacy; the tragedian dined with the poet, was introduced to his friends, and on nights when he did not
play accompanied him to his private box at the theatre,
where Mrs. Inchbald was asked by Rogers to meet
these famous men. Lord Essex likewise entertained

Kean, and was desirous of breaking him from his habit of drinking to excess, which sometimes was sadly visible. The number of those who asserted they had known Kean for years, had from the first foreseen his success, nay, helped him to achieve it, was marvellous. The world would be friendly with him, for he was a man destined to advance.

Amusing mistakes were, however, occasionally made by those who would laud him, or boast the possession of his friendship. Once when he was dining at the house of a noble lord, a famous barrister who was present assured Kean he had never seen acting until the previous evening, when he had been present at his representation of Richard III.

"Indeed," replied Kean quietly; "but surely you must have seen other actors."

"Yes," answered the legal luminary, "I have seen both Cooke and Kemble, but they must excuse me, Mr. Kean, if I should turn from them, and frankly say to you with Hamlet, 'Here's metal more attractive.'"

Kean, highly flattered, smiled pleasantly, and begged to have the honour of drinking a glass of wine with this discriminating gentleman. The discourse soon after turned on a curious law-suit that had been decided during a recent circuit, on which the barrister had been engaged, when Kean, after some consideration, inquired if he had ever visited the Exeter Theatre.

"Very rarely indeed," was the answer, "though, by the bye, now I recollect, during the last assizes I dropped in towards the conclusion of *Richard III.* Richmond was played by a very promising young actor, but such a Richard! such a harsh, croaking, barn-brawler! I forget his name, but—"

"I'll tell it you," said the little man, rising and tapping the speaker on the shoulder, "I'll tell it you—his name was Kean."

In the laugh which followed Kean heartily joined, and laughed all the louder when the critic said, "How much and how rapidly you have improved."

On another occasion the tragedian had likewise the benefit of hearing himself described in a manner even less flattering. It happened one afternoon he and his friend Jack Hughes, to whom, by the way, he presented a ring value one hundred pounds as a memento of their friendship, dropped into Offey's tavern in Henrietta Street, Covent Garden, to enjoy a good glass and a quiet chat. Seated in a snug box in one corner of the apartment, they soon became aware of a loud-voiced, swaggering, garrulous, red-headed fellow who was entertaining a circle of admirers. This was one Woolson, a wholesale tobacconist, who delighted in narrating gossip, and figuring as the hero of his own tales. Kean, whose appearance at this time was not generally known off the stage, heard his name mentioned by Woolson, and listened to his conversation.

"It is true enough," he said, nodding his head, "Dr. Drury brought him to town; he talked with me on the subject, in fact, we went together in Dorsetshire to see him act. I shall never forget Kean's gratitude when we proposed his appearance at Drury Lane."

Kean, thrusting himself forward, gazed in amazement at the speaker, but did not interrupt him. More was to follow.

"I saw him to-day in Cecil Street," continued Woolson; "he is in the very ecstasy of triumph. But I'm afraid my friend has something yet to learn," he added mysteriously.

"How; what is that?" demanded the listening group.

"Why, he neglects his wife, a most kind and amiable woman, and, as the poet declares—

> ' That one error
> Fills him with faults.' "

A murmur of applause followed this quotation, and each man looked wise. Kean, boiling with passion, would have leapt forward, but Hughes held him back, and Woolson, unconscious of his danger, leisurely continued, as he pulled a little snuff-box from his pocket—

"This was his—a slight token of his obligation to me, as he was pleased to say. I carry it for his sake."

"Do you, by the gods," cried Kean, frantic with rage, as he sprang from his corner, snatched the snuff-box, and flung it through a pane of glass into the street.

Sudden consternation fell upon Woolson and his admirers, who, when they had somewhat recovered, rose to avenge their friend; but Kean with a dramatic gesture waved them back, and then, folding his arms on his breast, said, "Behold! I am Edmund Kean." Then turning his flashing eyes on Woolson he hissed out one word, "Slanderer!"

Believing him a rank impostor, they rushed upon the little tragedian, beat him with violence, and turned him from the house; Hughes likewise shared his fate, and moreover lost a shoe in the fray.

The season at Drury Lane wore on. Towards the end of May Kean took his first London benefit, playing for the occasion the character of Luke in *Riches, or the Wife and Brother*, an alteration of Massinger's *City Madam*. On the evening of this performance his friends and admirers filled the house, and vast numbers were turned from the doors. A brace of poets, Lord Byron and Thomas Moore, occupied a box, whilst every other in the house was crowded to suffocation; but Byron vowed he would enjoy Kean's acting uninterrupted, and had unceremoniously left a party made up for the occasion. This benefit, including monetary gifts presented him, after the fashion of the times, brought Kean the sum of eleven hundred and fifty pounds. The world went well with him now. A friend who had known him in the days of his adversity, calling on him soon after his benefit had been announced, was struck by the change in his circumstances.

"I do not exaggerate," he writes, "when I say that money was lying about the room in all directions; the present Mr. Charles Kean, then a fine little boy with rich curling hair, was playing with some score of guineas (then a rare coin) on the floor; bank-notes were in heaps on the mantel-piece, table, and sofa; and poor Mrs. Kean was quite bewildered with plans of the house and applications. I remember three ladies being intro- duced, who approached Mrs. Kean as if she were a divinity. Little Charles had deserted his guineas, and mounted himself on a wooden horse with stirrups.

'What a sweet child!' they whispered, and eyed him as if he had been a young prince."

Drury Lane Theatre closed for the summer season on the 16th of July, 1814, when Kean played Richard III. The wild enthusiasm displayed by the audience remained long in the memory of those present. In the course of six months he had acted sixty-eight times, and represented six different characters. The profits he had gained were great, but those he had brought to the shareholders of the theatre were greater yet. On the evenings he played, thirty-two thousand nine hundred and forty-two pounds, twelve shillings and sixpence had been taken at the doors—almost five hundred pounds nightly at an average. Presently at a meeting of shareholders, the chairman, Mr. Whitbread, spoke of "the incomparable performer Mr. Kean, by whose deserved attraction, after one hundred and thirty-five nights of continued loss, their interests had been retrieved." Mr. Whitbread's oratory savoured of the eloquence of an after dinner speech. The extra-ordinary powers of this eminent actor, he said, had, as might well be imagined, drawn forth the criticisms of all theatrical amateurs and judges; and though there might be some few who did not agree with him in regarding Mr. Kean as the most shining actor that had appeared in the theatrical world for many years, yet he was happy to find that the general opinion concurred with his own in this respect. Reference was made by the chairman to the wonderful force, energy, and truth of the tragedian's representations, of the emotions he excited, the sympathy he gained, the power he displayed, to which the town fully, if not universally, assented.

He had verily become the fashion. His portrait was painted by Halls, prints of him were exhibited in shop windows, poems lauding him appeared in the papers; and Hazlitt tells us, "If you had not been to see the little man twenty times in Richard, and did not deny his being hoarse in the last act, or admire him for being so, you were looked on as a lukewarm devotee, or half an infidel!

CHAPTER VII.

DURING the summer months Edmund Kean played at
Bristol, Gloucester, Birmingham, and Dublin. His
fame travelling before him gained him enthusiastic
receptions. Jones, the manager of the Dublin Theatre,
who two years previously had refused him an engagement at three pounds a week, was now glad to share
the receipts of the house with him after deducting
eighty pounds for expenses. At Birmingham he was
hailed with great delight. The exchequer of Elliston's
Theatre was, as he wittily said, "becoming shaky, and
presenting a drunken account, which could hardly keep
a balance." The melodramas and tragedies which had

recently been presented on his boards had met with such sad fate at the hands of his actors, that a wag had written in large letters on the stage door " Mangling done here." Furthermore, Elliston and his theatre had been dealt severe blows from the pulpit of a Presbyterian minister, a man this merry manager called John *Knocks.* But on Kean's arrival no fear was entertained that tragedy would be barbarously murdered; and the wrathful preacher was forsaken in favour of the popular actor.

Drury Lane Theatre opened on the 20th of September, 1814, with the comedy of *The Rivals.* The interior had been reconstructed and redecorated with classic figures, golden scrolls, and brilliant foliage, the whole surmounted by a ceiling representing " blue skies fading into distance." The audience filling the house on the night when such splendour was first revealed to public eyes, was so greatly impressed by the effect when the lights were raised, and the glory of their surroundings became plain to their sight, that they testified their delight by four rounds of applause; and yet another round followed when the green curtain drew up and revealed a new drop-scene, representing the ruins of a classic temple, whose reflection was mirrored in an azure lake, whilst a milk-white goat grazed upon verdant pasture in the distance. Then the orchestra struck up *God Save the King*, which was interrupted by cries of "Song, song," in answer to which the drop-scene rose, and the whole company came forward to sing the National Anthem. And a sense of loyalty—which now seems antiquated—being satisfied, the comedy began.

Not until the 3rd of October did Kean appear for the first time this season, when he played Richard III. in a manner that made Coleridge say, "Seeing him act was like reading Shakespeare by flashes of lightning." The public whilst witnessing his performances with unabated interest, yet looked forward eagerly to his representation of a new character. Accordingly it was announced that on the 5th of November (1814) he would appear as Macbeth. It was asserted by the adherents of the Kemble school, that as the Thane Kean must assuredly fail. He wanted height and dignity of presence, two prominent advantages that Kemble had; but what the elder tragedian lacked, Kean possessed. The play was mounted with an accuracy to detail and liberal expenditure seldom witnessed at this period on any stage. Locke's music was introduced, a new overture and symphonies composed, and fresh scenery painted. On the evening of the performance not merely the boxes, circles, pit, and gallery were full, but the lobbies and passages were crowded by those satisfied merely to hear Kean's voice. He was, *Bell's Weekly Messenger* states, "greeted with rapture, and attention seemed to wait upon him with breathless expectation."

The small stature and slight build of the man were lost sight of and forgotten in the display of power, horror, and ambition he presented. In the murder scene he exerted the full force of his genius in representing the workings of Macbeth's mind. One who was present wrote, that "as a lesson of common humanity it was heart-rending. The hesitation, the bewildered look, the coming to himself when he sees his hands bloody, the manner in which his voice clung to his throat and choked his utterance, his agony and tears, the force of nature overcome by passion, beggared description. It was a scene which no one who saw it can ever efface from his recollection."

The Covent Garden company had during the early part of the year seen with certain dismay Kean's assured success. Kemble, Young, and Mrs. Jordan had put forth their strength in vain, for the popularity of the new tragedian more than counterbalanced the merits of old favourites; and whilst Drury Lane

Theatre had been crowded to its uttermost limits, the rival house was but thinly peopled. It therefore became the policy of the managers to remedy this condition of affairs, but the means were difficult to obtain. To search through the provinces for a promising young tragedian, and produce him as a rival to Kean, would have been an indignity intolerable to Kemble; it was therefore resolved to seek an actress who, by force of her talents, might divide public attraction with Kean. Fortunately for the manager, the search was of short duration, for at this time the fame of a young actress named O'Neill, then playing in Dublin, crossed the Channel.

Elizabeth O'Neill was the daughter of a poor Irish player, who, marrying early in life, had become the father of a numerous family. For years he had strolled from town to town in his native country, meeting various degrees of hardship, and battling hourly with unkindly fortune. For a time he had managed a company, poor as himself in pocket, yet rich in hopes as he, and played with them in barns and out-houses, in town-halls and country mansions, sharing such gains as fell to his lot amongst his threadbare troop. Life's shifting scenes brought them light and shadow, joy and pain. Eventually better luck befell him, and he was engaged as acting manager to the Drogheda Theatre. At this town his little blue-eyed daughter Betty, then about twelve years of age, was for the first time sent to school; and here, when she was in the zenith of her fame, were many who remembered "the purty little crayther runnin' barefoot about the streets." Even then her beauty was remarkable, a subtle grace and natural refinement marked her movements, her fair face was bright with intelligence.

Whenever juvenile characters were required in the pieces performed at the Drogheda Theatre, little Betty was trained to fill them, and played with so much sense and sympathy, that she won unusual applause from her kindly audiences. As she grew in years she acted more important parts with equal success, so that it happened when Talbot, then manager of the Belfast Theatre, saw her performing, he immediately engaged her to play heroines at his house. With the constant practise and wider opportunities this stage gave her, progress became rapid, and her popularity grew apace.

At this period Miss Walstein, a clever and experienced player, known as the Hibernian Siddons, was the leading actress of Crow Street Theatre, Dublin. Her admirers were many and her attractions great, aware of which, and fancying her services could not be dispensed with, she wrote to the manager shortly before the beginning of a certain season, that unless she received an increase of salary and other privileges she would no longer consent to remain a member of his company. And his finances not warranting him to comply with her demands, he feared his theatre must remain closed. MacNally the box-keeper, hearing this, said it would be a pity to shut the doors when he had a remedy at hand, if he chose to avail himself of it; and on being asked what he meant, MacNally replied—

"The girl who has been so strongly recommended to you as a promising actress is now in Dublin with her father, on their way to his theatre in Drogheda. I have heard it said by those who have seen her that she plays Juliet well, and is very young and pretty. I'm sure she would be delighted to have the opportunity of appearing before a Dublin audience, and, if you please, I will make her the proposal."

Delighted by the prospect of securing her, the manager bade him immediately seek her, and MacNally started at once for her lodgings, where he found the lovely Juliet frying herrings for her father's dinner. To her MacNally, a little round-faced, stout-legged gentleman dressed in black, with silk stockings, pumps, and powdered hair, was a veritable angel of light bearing a message of gladness. She eagerly accepted the offer made her, appeared the following Saturday evening at Crow Street, captivated the town, and took the first decisive step towards fame and fortune.

Presently Miss Walstein returned to Crow Street, but her young rival divided popularity with her. A friend of Elliston's, writing to him in 1813, when he was about to open the Olympic, speaks of Miss O'Neill as an actress of great promise. "She is most deservedly a high favourite with the Dublin audience. Her line is tragedy and leading comedy. Her performance the other night of Mrs. Oakley was quite first-rate. In sensibility she is indeed 'for tenderness formed.' In the affair of the heart she touches nearer than Mrs. Siddons. I now believe in Thespis and his adventures, for this lady first acted in a stable."

On the first occasion of her playing Juliet in the Irish capital, the balcony scene, in which she most excelled, lost much of its romance in consequence of a remark hurled from the gods. Owing to the limited size of the stage, the balcony was unusually low, whilst

Conway, who played Romeo, was six feet two inches in height.   In delivering the lines—

> "Oh, that I were a glove upon that hand,
>   That I might touch that cheek,"

he laid his elbow on the balcony, whereon a fellow in the gallery, despising the lover's timidity, cried out, "Get out wid your blarney now, why don't ye touch her then, and don't be praching," a remark that convulsed the house with laughter.

Such had been the early career of the young actress to whom Harris now offered an engagement at Covent Garden Theatre, at an increasing salary of fifteen, sixteen, and eighteen pounds a week.   This proposal was joyfully and gratefully accepted, and her first appearance in London was fixed for the 6th of October, 1814, when it was announced she was to play Juliet.   For weeks previous rumours of her beauty and genius were spread through the town; the press hinted of the treat in store for the public; those who had seen her acting in Ireland predicted her triumph in England.   Another Siddons, it was said, had risen to delight her generation ; expectation rose ; enthusiasm spread.

Early in the afternoon of the 6th of October, the various entrances to Covent Garden Theatre were surrounded by crowds determined to obtain admission;

and the doors being opened at half-past five, an immense throng poured into the house, and rushed into the pit and galleries. Soon after the boxes and circles were filled, and a brilliant audience impatiently waited for the curtain to rise. Amongst those present on this evening was William Macready, a young actor, who at the same theatre was soon to cause an excitement little less than that he now witnessed.

Presently the play began, and the audience eagerly waited the entrance of the new Juliet, who in due time rushed upon the stage in obedience to her nurse's call, when, such was the impression her youthful charm and exceeding beauty made, that the whole house rose to greet her. Never, perhaps, had an actress so lovely and graceful been seen. Slightly above the middle height, her figure was perfectly moulded, lithe, and sinuous; her blue eyes were gentle and tender in expression; her features, though not regular, reflected every emotion; her forehead was crowned by masses of auburn hair. "The charming picture she presented," says Macready, "was one that time could not fade from my memory. It was not altogether the matchless beauty of form and face, but the spirit of perfect innocence and purity that seemed to glisten in her speaking eyes, and breathe from her chiselled lips." Then in her twenty-third year, she looked scarce more than fifteen, and was an ideal Juliet. Her joyous laugh came straight from her heart, her voice sounded with delicious music that might have rang through the green glades of Arcadia, her. step was buoyant, her every movement picturesque. In the early scenes of the play her acting was considered by one critic as too light and playful; but the outburst of girlish spirit betrayed was doubtless intended to contrast the thoughtfulness and fervour which succeeded her meeting with Romeo. From that moment a new principle, too deep for words, over subtle for thought, became part of her life ; her love, the mere growth of an hour, coloured existence, and the old careless mirth of the past departed from her ways.

Perhaps the greatest fascination she exercised lay in the naturalness of her acting. Passages and scenes were given with a beauty and simplicity that depended on the feelings of the moment for effect, and which study alone could never produce. A sense of innate delicacy, of rare sensibility glowing through the fervour of her words, and the presence of passion subdued by modesty, rendered her performance a delight to behold. One of the critics present wrote, that " In the silent expression of feeling we have seldom witnessed anything finer than her acting, when she is told of Romeo's death, her listening to the friar's story of the poison, and her change of manner towards the nurse when she advises her to marry Paris. Her delivery of the speeches in the scenes where she laments Romeo's banishment, and anticipates his waking in the tomb, marked the fine play and undulation of natural sensibility rising and falling with the gusts of passion, and at last worked up into an agony of despair, in which imagination approaches the brink of frenzy."

No such Juliet had ever been seen upon the English stage, and her audience, dazzled by such loveliness and grace, moved by such tenderness and force, burst into a wild tumult of applause when the curtain fell. And when this enthusiasm had after many minutes subsided, and another play was announced for the following evening, *Romeo and Juliet* was demanded by hundreds of voices, to which command the manager yielded. Crowds were nightly turned from the doors when she played; her original agreement was cancelled, a salary of thirty pounds a week given her, and her name was lauded by the town.

More touching and powerful was her performance of Belvidera in *Venice Preserved*, which character she acted on the 13th of the month. Her sorrow and despair wrung tears from her audiences, even critics wept, and at the close of the last act women fainted, and were carried to their carriages in hysterics. Her success now equalled that which had attended Mrs. Siddons in her palmy days, and it was said in her scenes of tenderness and grief she excelled that great actress.

But her Juliet, which she repeated again and again, remained a favourite, and shared popularity with Kean's Othello, Richard, and Macbeth. It therefore occurred to the Drury Lane management, that it would be well to produce *Romeo and Juliet*, with Kean as the lover. To this proposal he was averse, knowing his power lay in portraying hate, ambition, remorse, or revenge rather than the gentler passion. However, he allowed himself · to be persuaded into playing Romeo, Mrs. Bartley being the Juliet, and the tragedy being carefully rehearsed, was produced on the 2nd of January, 1815. The result could not, in comparison with his other characters, be considered a success. His performance was certainly unequal, in the passages requiring tenderness—especially in the balcony scene he was considered cold and unimpressive; but in his fight with Tybalt, his interview with Friar Laurence, and his death, he showed a true conception of the part, and a perfect mastery of his art. Hazlitt found words of praise for him. "In the midst of the extravagant and irresistible expression

of Romeo's grief at being banished from this object
of his love," says this critic, "his voice suddenly stops
and falters, and is choked with sobs of tenderness when
he comes to Juliet's name. Those persons must be
made of stronger stuff than ourselves who are proof
against Mr. Kean's acting, both in this scene and the
dying convulsions at the close. His repetition of the
word *banished* is one of the finest pieces of acting the
modern stage can boast."

He appeared as Romeo but twelve times, and then
came a fresh desire on the part of the public to see him
in some new part. With the committee of management lay the selection of pieces to be produced, and
the various tastes of these gentlemen, together with
the character of the manuscripts submitted to them,
rendered a decision difficult. An amusing account of
the troubles they encountered is given in a letter
written by Lord Byron to his friend Tom Moore.
"When I belonged to the Drury Lane Committee,"
he says, "and was one of the Sub-Committee of
Management, the number of plays upon the shelves
was about five hundred. Conceiving that amongst
these there must be some of merit, in person and by
proxy I caused an investigation. I do not think that
of those which I saw there was one which could be

conscientiously tolerated. There never were such things as most of them. Maturin was very kindly recommended to me by Walter Scott, to whom I had recourse —firstly, in the hope that he would do something for us himself; secondly, in despair, that he would point out to us any young (or old) writer of promise. Maturin sent his *Bertram*, and a letter without his address, so that at first I could give him no answer. When I at last hit upon his residence, I sent him a favourable answer, and something more substantial. His play succeeded; but I was at that time absent from England.

"I tried Coleridge too, but he had nothing feasible in hand at the time. Mr. Southeby obligingly offered all his tragedies, and I pledged myself; and, notwithstanding many squabbles with my committee brethren, did get *Ivan* accepted, read, and the parts distributed. But lo! in the very heart of the matter, upon some tepidness on the part of Kean, or warmth on that of the author, Southeby withdrew his play. Sir James Bland Burgess did also present four tragedies and a farce, and I moved green-room and Sub-Committee, but they would not.

"Then the scenes I had to go through—the authors and the authoresses, and the milliners, and the wild Irishmen—the people from Brighton, from Blackwall,

from Chatham, from Cheltenham, from Dublin, from
Dundee—who came in upon me, to all of whom it was
proper to give a civil answer, and a hearing, and a
reading. Mrs. Glover's father, an Irish dancing-master
of sixty years, calling upon me to request to play
Archer, dressed in silk stockings on a frosty morning
to show his legs (which were certainly good and Irish
for his age, and had been still better). Miss Emma
Somebody, with a play entitled *The Bandit of Bohemia*,
or some such title or production. Mr. O'Higgins, then
resident at Richmond, with an Irish tragedy, in which
the unities could not fail to be observed, for the pro-
tagonist was chained by the leg to a pillar during the
chief part of the performance. He was a wild man of
a salvage appearance, and the difficulty of *not* laughing
at him was only to be got over by reflecting upon the
probable consequences of such cachinnation. . . .

" Then the Committee ! then the Sub-Committee—we
were but few, but never agreed. There was Peter
Moore who contradicted Kinnaird, and Kinnaird who
contradicted everybody; then our two managers and
our secretary, and yet we were all very zealous, and in
earnest to do good, and so forth. George Lamb furnished
us with prologues to our revived old English plays, but
was not pleased with me for complimenting him as

'the Upton' of our theatre (Mr. Upton is or was the poet who writes the songs for Astley's), and almost gave up prologuing in consequence."

After much deliberation, it was ultimately agreed that Marlow's comedy of *Town and Country* should be put on the boards, Kean personating Ruben Glenroy. During this season he likewise represented Richard II. —a play which had lain unacted since the days of Shakespeare, until young Macready had two years previously produced it at the Newcastle Theatre,— Penruddock in the *Wheel of Fortune*, a comedy by Cumberland, Zanga in Dr. Young's tragedy of the *Revenge*, Abel Drugger in the *Alchemist*, and Octavian in the *Mountaineer*. In each of these characters he was fairly successful, especially in those dealing with tragedy. In comedy he was well appreciated, and his acting of Abel Drugger was declared by the press "an exquisite piece of ludicrous naïvete."

Kean had a more severe critic in Mrs. Garrick, who saw him act Abel Drugger on the 24th of May, when he took his benefit. On the following morning he received a note containing these words—

"DEAR SIR,

"You can't play Abel Drugger.

"Yours, E. GARRICK."

To which he promptly replied—

"DEAR MADAM,

"I know it.

"Yours, E. KEAN."

During a visit he subsequently paid her, Mrs. Garrick enlarged on the opinion she had already written to him, and dwelt on the merits of David in this character—his quaint voice, his comic expression, his droll gestures. Kean, feeling impatient at this eulogy, at length interrupted her by asking, "Could he sing?" to which, after a brief reflection, she answered, "No." "Well," said Kean, rising to depart, "I can."

This season he occasionally repeated his representations of the characters by which he had made his fame the previous year. One night whilst he played Richard III., William Macready, who had first seen him as Alonzo the Brave at the Birmingham Theatre, occupied a box at Drury Lane. Accompanied by his father, who had journeyed to town that he might secure the services of Kean and Miss O'Neill for a few nights during the vacation, young Macready, anxious to see the great tragedian in Richard III., took his place before the curtain rose. When presently "a little keenly visaged man rapidly bustled across the stage," Macready writes,

"I felt there was meaning in the alertness of his manner and the quickness of his step. As the play proceeded, I became more and more satisfied that there was a mind of no common order. In his angry complaining of nature's injustice to his bodily imperfections, as he uttered the line, 'To shrink my arm up like a withered shrub,' he remained looking on the limb for some moments with a sort of bitter discontent, and then struck it back in angry disgust. My father, who sat behind me, touched me and whispered, 'It's very poor.' 'Oh, no,' I replied, 'it is no common thing,' for I found myself stretching over the box to observe him. The scene with Lady Anne was entered on with evident confidence, and was well sustained, in the affected earnestness of penitence to its successful close. In tempting Buckingham to the murder of the children he did not impress me as Cooke was wont to do, on whom the sense of the crime was apparent in the gloomy hesitation with which he gave reluctant utterance to the deed of blood. Kean's manner was consistent with his conception, proposing their death as a political necessity, and sharply requiring it as a business to be done. In the bearing of the man throughout as the intriguer, the tyrant, and the warrior, he seemed never to relax the ardour of his pursuit, presenting the life of

the usurper as one unbroken whole, and closing it with
a death picturesquely and poetically grand. Many of
the Kemble school resisted conviction in his merits, but
the fact that he had made me feel was an argument to
enroll me with the majority on the indisputable genius
he displayed."

Kean was engaged to sup with Macready and his son,
then in his twenty-first year, at the York Hotel; and
when the curtain fell on the death of Richard, the provincial manager hastened to his inn, that he might be
there to receive his distinguished guest. Kean, attended by Pope, then a member of the Drury Lane
company, soon followed. "I need not say," writes
Macready the younger, " with what intense scrutiny I
regarded him as we shook hands on our mutual introduction. The mild and modest expression of his
Italian features, and his unassuming manner, which I
might perhaps justly describe as partaking in some
degree of shyness, took me by surprise, and I remarked
with special interest the indifference with which he
endured the fulsome flatteries of Pope. He was very
sparing of words during, and for some time after,
supper; but about one o'clock, when the glass had circulated pretty freely, he became animated, fluent, and
communicative. His anecdotes were communicated

with a lively sense of the ridiculous; in the melodies he sang there was a touching grace, and his powers of mimicry were most humorously or happily exerted in an admirable imitation of Braham; and in a story of Incledon acting Steady the Quaker at Rochester without any rehearsal—where, in singing the favourite air, 'When the lads of the village so merrily, O,' he heard himself, to his dismay and consternation, accompanied by a single bassoon,—the music of his voice, his perplexity at each recurring sound of the bassoon, his undertone maledictions on the self-satisfied musician, the peculiarity of his habits, all were hit off with a humour and an exactness that equalled the best display Mathews ever made, and almost convulsed us with laughter. It was a memorable evening, the first and last I ever spent in private with this extraordinary man."

Throughout the season Miss O'Neill shared the enthusiasm of the town with Kean, and both houses entered on a seemingly prosperous career. When they closed in summer Miss O'Neill went to the Edinburgh Theatre, of which Henry Siddons, son of the great tragic actress, was manager. On the night previous to her first performance the portico of the house was crowded by porters hired to secure places when the box-office opened next morning. Henry Siddons was to have sustained the leading characters, but an illness, which eventually proved fatal, prevented his design.

Meanwhile Kean crossed over to Dublin, and was there received by a stormy ovation. Night after night the theatre was crowded to excess. On taking his benefit in this city during his first visit an unpleasant occurrence had taken place. Numerous and early applications for seats had been made to the box-keeper, but that individual declared Mr. Kean had kept to him-self the privilege of letting all the boxes, that he might oblige his particular friends; and presently, when Kean desired to have some boxes, he was assured they had all been taken. The sole reason for such conduct on the box-keeper's part was to secure bribes from those willing to pay any price for places; but these not being generally offered, the theatre on the occasion of Kean's benefit was scarcely filled. An explanation followed, and the motive being discovered, the under-graduates of Trinity College, who were amongst Kean's warmest admirers, waited on him to know if he would wish the theatre to be pulled down. This he declined. But now when the time came for his second benefit, the students undertook its management, let the boxes and dress circles, and on the eventful evening stood at the doors to receive tickets. The result was a triumph for

Kean, for the house, as a young under-graduate boasted, "was fuller than it could hold."

Returning to town in the autumn, Kean took Lady Rycroft's furnished house at 12 Clarges Street, Piccadilly, where much good company flocked. Mrs. Kean, who was proud of her husband's fame, delighted in assembling people of title, fashion, and distinction round her board; but Kean, who was a born Bohemian, had no regard for rank or position, and rather endured than enjoyed the society of those who would have posed as his patrons. Such were not congenial to his temperament, and frequently when a brilliant party at his house had ended, he betook himself to a tavern, where with some old friends or kindred spirits he spent the night in drinking and smoking, listening to anecdote and song.

One of the favourite places of resort for himself and his friends was a public-house called the Coal-hole, situated in Fountain Court, off the Strand. This was the meeting-place of a club known as The Wolves, founded for the enjoyment of "good fellowship and harmony." Here all men, whosoever they were, met on terms of equality. Kean, speaking as chairman, hoped no one would enter "this circle of good fellows without a pride that ranks him with the courtier, or philosophy that

levels him with the peasant." He hoped that every
Wolf oppressed with worldly grievance, unmerited contumely, or unjust persecutions, would, with a heart
glowing with defiance, exclaim, " I'll to my brothers;
there I shall find ears attention to my tale of sorrow,
hands open to relieve, and close for my defence."

The Wolves, as the members of this club were called,
consisted of actors and those connected with theatres,
together with such merry souls as loved a strong glass
and a witty tale.   The attraction the Coal-hole possessed for Kean was fraught with evil.   Having reached
a height in his profession, which even in his most
sanguine hours he had not dreamt of attaining, lauded
by the public, appreciated by his friends, he no longer
practised the restraints which alone enabled him to
surmount his difficulties.   His success had not made
him mad, as he had predicted, but in his eyes it served
as a license for eccentric conduct, concerning which
various stories were afloat.

During the season he not only set up a carriage,
but purchased several valuable horses.   On one of
these, which he named Shylock, he would occasionally
mount on leaving the theatre or tavern, and ride reck-
lessly through the night, he knew not where, tearing
through streets, rushing along country roads, a modern

Herne the hunter, jumping toll-gates, flying past frightened peasants, outriding footpads in search of prey. Not until daybreak did horse and horseman return home, exhausted, and covered with mud or dust. Not satisfied with a fame such as few had enjoyed so early in life, he condescended to court notoriety, and in this was not a little aided by a tame American lion, given him by Sir Edward Tucker. Visitors at his house found him engaged in his drawing-room in educating this animal, and timidly shrank from making the acquaintance of the colossal pet, who might also be seen seated in the stern of a wherry which his master rowed up and down the Thames, to the admiration of many. Again the little tragedian was the observed of all observers as he rolled through the streets in his carriage drawn by four bays, wrapped in a great Spanish cloak, which Sir George Beaumont had brought from Seville, and presented to him. And to quell the constant craving for excitement, begotten of his artistic temperament, he frequented prize rings, and associated with boxers on most friendly terms.

Grattan, the officer to whom he had once taught fencing in Waterford, called on him in the spring of 1816, and no sooner had Kean learned his visitor's name, than he sprang down-stairs to greet him heartily, and honestly

welcome him. "Had he received the visit of a powerful patron or generous benefactor," Grattan writes, "he
could not, or at least need not, have shown more gratitude than he evinced at the recollection of my slight
services in passing some tickets for his Chimpanzee
benefit so long before. I consider," he adds, "this trait
in Kean's conduct a fair test of his character. It was
thoroughly disinterested, and was not a mere burst of
good feeling, nor a display of ostentation—for these
would have been sufficiently satisfied with a momentary expression. But his whole behaviour during a
couple of months that I remained in London at that
time was a continuance of friendly attentions. I dined
with him frequently, and met at his house much good
company. Persons of very high respectability, and
many of them of rank, were amongst his constant
guests. His dinners were excellent, but his style of
home living did not appear extravagant; and the
evening parties were extremely pleasant, with a great
deal of good music. Nothing could be more friendly
or hospitable than the conduct of the worthy hostess,
whom I had never formerly seen but in her solitary
exhibition at Waterford. She was in her own house,
and surrounded by everything that might dazzle the
mind's eye and dizzy the brain of almost any one,

a fair specimen of natural character. Her head was
evidently turned by all her husband's fame and her
own finery, and their combined consequences were
visibly portrayed in her looks, and bodied forth with
exquisite naïvete. But there was withal a shrewdness,
an off-handedness, and tact quite Irish; and what was
still more so, a warm-hearted and overflowing recog-
nizance of ever so trivial a kindness or tribute of
admiration offered to Edmund before he became a
great man."

One evening when Kean was not performing, Grattan
invited him to dinner at the Sabloniere Hotel in
Leicester Square, to meet a couple of friends. At six
o'clock Kean's carriage came rattling up to the door,
and the tragedian descended, dressed in a silk-lined
coat, white breeches, and buckled shoes. Before sitting
down to table, he informed his host that he had an
engagement at nine to attend a party where he was
particularly expected. The dinner was choice, the
company witty, the wine excellent, and Kean, still
enjoying himself when the hour mentioned arrived,
tarried awhile. Presently word was brought the horses
were waiting, but he did not stir; later, messengers
arrived from those who were expecting him, but they
had no power to move him. Decanters passed freely

round, stories were told, songs sung, imitations of famous actors given, and it was not until the clock struck midnight he rose to depart.

Expressing his unwillingness that they should separate, he invited the party to accompany him, without mentioning the destination to which he was bound. Unhesitatingly they assented, for at this period of the entertainment they would readily have followed him to the end of the world. Accordingly these four got into Kean's carriage, which had been waiting over three hours, and drove rapidly until the horses stopped at the head of a narrow passage leading from the Strand. Down this they tottered, bumping now and then against the walls, until they arrived at the open doors of a tavern, from which lights flashed and noises sounded. A score of waiters and women struggled forward to see the great actor as he took his unsteady way up-stairs, followed by his friends. Reaching large folding doors at the end of a corridor on the first floor, he dashed at them violently, and flinging them wide, entered the room amidst roars of applause.

Here, seated at a long supper-table, were about sixty men; beyond that fact all was a blaze of lights, a confusion of mirrors and decanters, a kaleidoscope of human faces, and a Babel of numerous voices to the visitors.

No sooner, however, were they noticed by the company, than a loud murmur of disapprobation arose, expostulations and explanations ensued, which ended in Kean and his three friends being hurriedly led to an adjoining room, where it was stated a violent outrage on the society of the Wolves had been committed by the grand master and founder in admitting strangers without a formal introduction, and the only means of repairing this breach of the laws was to make the visitors members. Accordingly they were obliged to take an oath, the object of which they scarce knew, sign their names as well as they were able in a register, and pay fees of a few guineas. Then being announced members of the club, they returned to the large room, when Kean took the chair reserved for him at the head of the table, and his health being drank he made a florid speech. Bottles were passed round, voices grew more confused, the lights more dazzling, until at last all ended in oblivion to the new-made Wolves, and henceforth the night became to them as the memory of a dream.

Amongst those who visited Kean at this time were two pugilists, known as Mendoza and Richmond the Black, with whom he was wont to try his skill as a boxer in his dining-room. To witness a match between

two champions named Curtis and West-country Dick,
soon to lose his life in a prize-fight, he on one occasion
took his friend Grattan. The spot selected for this so-
called sport was situated some ten miles outside town,
and was crowded by men of position and rank, young
bloods, university men, and sporting characters of all
degrees in the social circle. Kean on his arrival was
received with the honours due to a liberal patron and
a distinguished amateur, and ushered into a space
close beside the combatants, where he introduced such
lights of the ring as Scroggings, Crib, and Oliver to
his companion. The air was rife with excitement;
wagers were laid; deeds of prowess in the past recounted;
victory and defeat freely predicted for this hero or that
favourite. Then the ring was cleared, the fight began;
skill was cheered, falls were received with groans, blood
freely spouted, and the fighters pounded each other's
faces out of all semblance to humanity, whilst their
admirers looked on in high glee.

Kean was now a social lion, and as such many a
noble dame sought to lure him to her drawing-room
menagerie. But he, gauging the value of such honours,
boasted that he refused their invitations and despised
their patronage. The only man of title in whose
society he found pleasure was Lord Byron; and he

not only admired, but. it was said, in despising public opinion, accentuating his eccentricities, and occasionally allowing himself to be weighed down by melancholy moods, imitated the poet. Both had something more than genius in common; both flashed through their spheres like brilliant meteors; both ended their careers in the prime of an existence whose last days were clouded with sorrow.

Byron not merely admired the tragedian, but, conscious of the many good traits underlying his character, esteemed him as a man. He had previously hoped that by getting him into good society he would be prevented from falling like George Frederick Cooke, whose intemperance caused his ruin; and accordingly the poet sought to attach Kean to his own circle. In this he was not successful. The great actor was shy and uneasy in the company of men of position or intellect, and felt far more at home in a tavern with his brethren of the sock and buskin. Again and again the poet, whose circle was composed of those whose talents recommended themselves to him, endeavoured to include Kean amongst his associates, but in vain. A short time before Byron left his native land for ever, he invited the tragedian to dinner, that he might meet Lord Kinnaird, just returned from Greece. A few men distinguished in various ways were to complete the party. It so happened that on the evening fixed for this feast of reason and flow of wine, Kean had already accepted an invitation from Charles Incledon to join some friends at supper at Cribb's tavern in Panton Street, Haymarket, and had promised to take the chair on the occasion. Incledon, it will be remembered, had acted kindly by Kean when he was a friendless lad, and the tragedian never forgot a friend or a foe. Therefore when Byron requested he would dine with him, Kean excused himself on the plea of a previous engagement, but Byron insisted he must come and meet his friends. Accordingly Kean promised he should be present, and on the appointed evening sat down at the poet's pleasant board. But neither the company nor the conversation had much attraction for him, he remained silent and restrained, and soon after dessert had been served, slipped quietly out of the room. For a while he was not missed, but presently Byron, noting an empty chair, inquired where his friend had gone; to which the servants replied, Mr. Kean had kept his carriage waiting from the time he entered the house, and had now driven away.

On another occasion, at a dinner given by Lord Hertford, Kean was asked to meet the Duke of Beaufort,

Lord Glengall, Sir George Warrender, Douglas Kinnaird, Francis Russell, and some others. In order to make the great actor more at his ease, his friend and fellow-player Oxberry was likewise invited, and with him Kean duly arrived. The tragedian was the hero of the hour; wine was drank with him, compliments paid him, his conversation was courted. And it being known that he could be entertaining and witty when he pleased, a pleasant evening was expected; but so far as Kean was concerned, their hopes were doomed to disappointment, for whilst the servants were removing the cloth he nodded to Oxberry, who approached him. "A couple of years ago," he said, "not one of these lords would have noticed the poor stroller, now their admiration is unbounded. Pshaw! I prefer a quiet glass with a friend like you to all their champagne, effervescent like themselves—let us go." And, unobserved by their host, they quietly left the room, and were soon on their way to a tavern.

Henry Crabb Robinson remembered meeting him at a gathering at Sergeant Rough's, a legal light who had married a daughter of the famous John Wilkes. This worthy man and his spouse delighted in entertaining literary and artistic society, and in their drawing-room might be met Flaxman the sculptor, a grotesque, hump-backed little man; Mrs. Abingdon, a contemporary of Garrick and Reynolds, now in the autumn of her days, but in the full enjoyment of life; gentle Charles Lamb and his sister Mary; William Godwin, author of *Caleb Williams*, on which the play of the *Iron Chest* was founded; Samuel Coleridge, William Wordsworth, Horne Tooke, Northcote the painter, Hazlitt the critic, and others of like distinction. Henry Crabb Robinson says the tragedian scarcely spoke; he was not at home in such company. "He has certainly a fine eye," he writes, " but his features were relaxed as if he had undergone great fatigue. When he smiles his look is rather constrained than natural. He is but a small man, and from the gentleness of his manners no one would anticipate the actor who excels in bursts of passion."

Lord William Lennox narrates a story in which Kean appears to better advantage. One summer month Earl Fitzhardinge proposed to give a dinner at the Old Ship Hotel, Greenwich, to Kean and a few of the tragedian's ardent admirers; and Kean having accepted the proposal, it was decided the guests should arrive at four o'clock at Berkeley House, Spring Gardens, Lord Fitzhardinge's residence, and drive from there to Greenwich in carriages. At the hour mentioned all those

invited arrived save Kean, from whom a note was
brought, regretting that sudden indisposition prevented
his attending.   Lord William Lennox, believing Kean's
absence was caused rather by his will than by his
health, drove at once to his house, and found him
perfectly well.   He then urged him to join the party,
which was arranged for him, stating that those invited
were his friends, and that the disappointment his absence
would cause his host would be great.

Eventually persuaded into compliance, Kean got into
the Victoria waiting him at the door, drove to Berkeley
House, and from there to Greenwich.   Having visited
the fine picture-gallery of the Hospital, the company
sat down to a dinner which proved very merry to all.
When the cloth had been removed, and the wine had
circulated freely, Kean began to talk.   Those around
him were sympathetic and laudatory, and he spoke
freely, describing his early career, when he had been
set down as a mere ranter, the hardships he suffered in
strolling, the fatigue he had endured in playing Shylock and harlequin, Macbeth and Tom Tug, on the
same evening to a gallery of twenty and a pit numbering half a score of rustics.   Then pressed by those
around him, he recited some of the speeches from the
Merchant of Venice, spoke soliloquies from *Macbeth* and

Othello, his dark eyes flashing, his breast heaving, then sang a song with sweetness and expression, gave imitations of some of the London actors, narrated green-room anecdotes that set the table in a roar, and finally turned somersaults as a harlequin. And so the hours wore away amidst merriment and laughter, song and story, until it was close upon midnight, when host and guests returned to their carriages, and drove home in the peaceful moonlight of a summer night.

Paul Bedford, the veteran actor, gives us a picture of Kean enjoying a little supper at the home of Andrew Ducrow, whose marvellous acts of horsemanship and elegant tight-rope dancing drew crowds from all parts of the town to Astley's. Ducrow was not only a great artist, but a hospitable host, and loved to gather round his board men of parts and wit. To meet Kean one night he had bidden Count D'Orsay, Nathan the composer, Sir George Wombwell, and Lord Adolphus FitzClarence, son of Mrs. Jordan and the Duke of Clarence. In such society Kean enjoyed himself, listening to the Count's *bon mots*, to Nathan's singing, to his host's narratives of his hair-breadth escapes on horse and rope; in return for which he sang and recited, to the delight of his hearers.

CHAPTER VIII.

WHILST Kean's private life gave great pleasure and some regret to his friends, his public career continued to afford infinite satisfaction to the public. During his third season he played Bajazet in *Tamerlane*, Aranza in the *Honeymoon*, Sir Giles Overreach in *A New Way to Pay Old Debts*, Sforza in the *Duke of Milan*, Bertram in the *Tragedy of Bertram*, and Kitely in *Every Man in his Humour*.

The most successful of all these representations was his Sir Giles Overreach. This drama of Massinger's was revived on the 12th of January, 1816, and great were the results expected from Kean's performance. Anticipation did not exceed them; no finer conception of villainy, no more forcible portrayal of passions, no greater acting had been seen upon the English stage. His performance of Sir Giles long remained a theme for praise and wonder. The last scene, for which the actor had reserved his strength, "was indeed," said the *Morning Chronicle*, "a climax of terrible destruction and awful desolation of a mind buoyed up by false hopes, the failure of which overwhelms it in blank desperation and universal wretchedness." The effect of this powerful playing was such, that one of the actresses on the stage, Mrs. Glover, overcome with fright at the horror depicted on his countenance, fainted; Byron at the same time was seized in his box by a convulsive fit; whilst women went into hysterics, and the whole house burst into a wild clamour of applause.

As Kean, breathless with fatigue and excitement, was passing to his dressing-room, he felt a hand grasp his shoulder, and turning round, saw Byron, yet pale from the effect of his fit. "Great! great!" said the poet; "that was acting! But hang it, you should not have treated me so scurvily by running from my dinner-table to Cribb's."   Kean in a few words apologized and explained, and after some months of coolness they were friends once more.   That evening's performance added a fresh leaf to his laurels.   Not since he had played Richard III. had he achieved such a triumph.   Returning home, he told his wife the scene he had witnessed— the sea of eager faces, the storm of excitement, the outburst of approbation.   "And what did Lord Essex say?" she interrupted him to ask.   "Damn Lord Essex; the pit rose at me," he replied.

This representation, which was "without doubt the most terrific exhibition of human passion that has been witnessed upon the modern stage," became the talk of all classes.   The few who had before considered the want of tragic strut and measured declamation in Kean's acting as absence of dignity and propriety, were now overwhelmed by the touches of nature and force of passion he displayed.   His praise was in all men's mouths.   "Mr. Kean," said the play-bill announcing his second representation of Sir Giles, "was honoured with the most enthusiastic applause, and the play having been received throughout with distinguished approbation, and announced for repetition with unanimous approval, will be acted again on Monday and Friday."   On Monday over three hundred persons were

refused admission, so crowded was the house. The receipts of the night were five hundred and forty-seven
pounds; on the third evening's performance of the play,
five hundred and eighty pounds were taken at the
doors; on the fourth night these receipts were increased
by ten pounds; whilst on the fifth and sixth they
amounted to six hundred and nine pounds, the largest
sum taken during the season.

Indeed, the play brought such profit to the treasury,
and such honour to Kean, that the committee decided
on producing another of Massinger's plays, and the
Duke of Milan was accordingly announced for representation on the 9th of March. Kean spent much time in
studying his part, but though he played it well, the
drama had not sufficient interest to ensure its success.
On the night of its first performance, Lord William
Lennox narrates that, having dined with a couple of
friends, they proceeded to Drury Lane Theatre. As
they entered a narrow passage leading to the private
boxes, he heard a voice calling to the box-keeper that
sounded familiar, and saw a figure muffled in a great
cloak; recognizing Lord Byron, to whom he had previously been introduced, he bowed to the poet, who slightly
acknowledged his salute, and immediately disappeared
in the crowd. Setting down the poet as a capricious

mortal, Lord William and his friends entered their box, and watched the play with interest.   As the curtain fell upon the second act, the box-keeper handed Lord William a note containing these words—"The bearer will bring you to my den; till we meet breathe not the name of B."   Leaving his friends, he followed his guide to the entrance of a little box close to the orchestra, upon entering which he was warmly greeted by Byron, who said—

"I have a thousand apologies to make for the cut direct I was obliged to give you.   The fact is, I am here *incog.*; a relative died last week, and I ought to be at home, 'in sullen black and sackcloth.'   My father-in-law would be shocked if he heard that I did not stay at home for Bell's, I mean Lady Birron's (so he pronounced it), uncle.   You know that I am now Benedick the married man.   But sit down in front, and hear Kean's impassioned tones.   I must remain in my nook, or to-morrow we shall read in some of the morning papers of 'heartless conduct,' and 'atrocious outrage upon decency.'

Lord William was about to rise at the end of the third act, when the box-door opened, and Douglas Kinnaird entered.   After an introduction had taken place, the latter said,

"What a glorious house to-night! What will Whit-bread say? He and Cavendish Bradshaw were quite in despair on looking over the receipts of the off nights."

Presently Byron stated that his friend would like to see the green-room; "and as we gave out a particular order," he continued, "that no stranger should be admitted, perhaps you will take him round."

"What a law-maker—a law-breaker," Kinnaird responded; "but if Lord William wishes to go I shall have great pleasure in escorting him." And away they went; but the great actor was not in the green-room, and they soon returned.

Kean had occasion to remember this play, from an unpleasant incident with which it was connected. It happened on the 26th of March, when the drama was announced for performance that evening, he with some pleasant friends and boon companions left town in the morning for Deptford, intending to dine there, and get back in time for his representation. The dinner was a success, and the day passed merrily enough; healths were proposed, toasts were drank, and the hour at which Kean should have started for town slipped by unnoticed. When at last it was remembered by one of his companions, he was neither able nor willing to leave the table. Those around him capable of thinking coherently, became fearful of the results of his indiscretion, and concocting a story, sent Kean's carriage in full haste to the theatre, bidding the servants say their master had been on his way to town, when the horses took fright at some geese by the roadside, near the inn at which he dined, ran away, upset the carriage, and flung the occupant out with such force as to dislocate his shoulder.

Meanwhile, a great audience had gathered at Drury Lane Theatre to see Kean. And as he did not appear in his dressing-room at his usual time, the managers became uneasy, and despatched messengers to his home, and to the various haunts where it was hoped he might be discovered. As the minutes passed, and the hour arrived for the curtain to rise, the house grew impatient, and hisses and hootings became general. At seven o'clock Rae came forward, seemingly in great distress, and stated Kean was nowhere to be found. He begged the indulgence of all present, and proposed to substitute another play for the *Duke of Milan*. This suggestion meeting with opposition, he retired, but soon after reappeared, and begged to know what was the pleasure of the house, when he was answered by a universal cry of "Wait, wait." The orchestra then played *God save the*

King, and some other airs, until Rae once more stood before the curtain. No tidings, he stated, had arrived of Mr. Kean; and at the same time he requested them to remember this was the first time that actor had ever kept them waiting a moment. He then asked if they would accept *What Next*, and *Ways and Means*, and *Fortune's Frolic*, instead of the play announced, and the audience agreeing, the first piece was begun without further delay.

When the curtain fell upon the last act of *Ways and Means*, a player named Barnard came forward, and announced that *A New Way to Pay Old Debts* would be performed on Thursday. The name of the play bringing the tragedian to mind, several voices cried out angrily, "Kean! where's Kean?" and this cry being taken up, the house was stirred to a state of excitement. When the storm had sufficiently abated to allow him being heard, Barnard stated no intelligence of Mr. Kean had been yet received, and then withdrew. *Fortune's Frolic* was played, and the evening's programme concluded.

Fear and anxiety now beset Kean's friends and admirers, but their suspense was somewhat relieved late at night, when messengers arrived with the story of the dislocated shoulder. Next morning the papers regretted the serious accident which had befallen the tragedian, and feared he would be prevented from fulfilling his professional duties for some time. The *Morning Post* set forward the following tale, which, as may be seen, greatly improved upon the original version. "He dined with a few friends at Woolwich on Tuesday," it stated, "from whence he set out at due time to be at the theatre by five o'clock. He reached Deptford about four, and here he experienced the same untoward kind of accident to which his brethren of the sock and buskin appear so long to have been unfortunately fated. Driving at a very quick pace, he was suddenly overturned, and falling with great violence upon the pavement, he had the misfortune to break his arm. His head also struck with such violence that he was completely stunned, and in this state was he conveyed to a neighbouring house; nor had he become sufficiently sensible of his situation to send off the necessary intimation of his accident to the theatre until a late hour yesterday morning. We are happy to be informed that he was last night considerably recovered, though in a state of most excruciating pain from the fracture of his arm. About a fortnight ago he had a very unpleasant dream, from which, weakly enough, he indulged in the gloomy augury that he should die on St. Patrick's day; nor was he satisfied of the error of this strange presentiment even when the date had passed over; but thought that the awful visitation, as it did not take place on the day of the new style, must be intended for that of the old style. We regret that any such notion as this should have been entertained in a mind otherwise so fine and superior, as we understand it even now continues to press heavily upon him, the time of dreadful foreboding not being yet arrived. To-morrow is the fearfully awaited day; and however ridiculous his apprehension, Mr. Kean's friends will do well to use every means of eradicating from his mind so strange and injurious an impression. In this event Richard will soon be himself again; and his faithful representation may for half a century to come enjoy the annual festivities of St. Patrick, to the happiness of his friends and the delight of the public."

The tidings of the accident having been delivered at the theatre, found their way to Mrs. Kean, who, in the fulness of her credulity, prepared to set out for Deptford in the morning. Accompanied by a surgeon and a couple of the Drury Lane actors, she reached her destination before midday; where soon after Mr. Whitbread, Sir Francis Burdett, and others of Kean's friends, anxious for his condition, arrived. In the morning the tragedian had recovered his senses, and felt shocked and shamed at discovering his situation. Those with whom he had made merry the previous day told him of the excuse they had sent to town, and assured him, as he valued public favour, he must act according to the story they had framed.

Therefore the village apothecary was summoned, who for a certain consideration lent himself to the deception, and bound Kean's shoulder and arm with linen cloths. His face was then whitened, the blinds of his bed-room windows drawn, and on his visitors being permitted to see him they beheld him lying in bed, seemingly in a state of suffering and exhaustion. Though the apothecary had forbidden any excitement, Kean, when his visitors had returned to town, assured his wife he would follow their example. Fearing the shaking and fatigue might exhaust him, she protested against this design, but he persisted, and eventually he was assisted to his carriage, propped up with pillows, and driven slowly to Clarges Street. Arriving there, he was carefully lifted out and carried to his bed-room. When left alone with his wife, he suddenly jumped up, and flung his bandaged arm about his head. Bewildered and frightened, she stared

at him, half fearing he had gone mad, until he laughingly declared all was well, and confessed the hoax
which his folly had obliged him to support. Appearances, however, had to be maintained, and he therefore
remained within doors a few days.

The accident was supposed to have taken place
on the 26th of March, but five days later he announced
his intention of playing at the theatre. However, lest
the public might grow suspicious at his sudden recovery,
it was prepared for his reappearance by the following letter written to the manager of the theatre,
and published in the papers with a few prefatory
remarks.

"The public will be glad to hear," said the *Morning
Post*, "that Mr. Kean was yesterday so far recovered
from the painful effects of his late accident, as to
induce a hope that that justly distinguished and most
favourite actor will be able to resume his professional
duties on Monday next; at least, such is the anxious
wish expressed by himself in the following letter of
yesterday's date to the managers of the theatre; and
we were further informed last night, that he felt
increased confidence in his ability to undertake the
task.

" ' *Clarges Street.*

" ' *To the Managers of Drury Lane Theatre.*

" ' GENTLEMEN,

" ' I beg you to accept, and convey to the Sub-Committee, my sincere thanks for the interest so kindly expressed for my recovery, and for the liberality with which I am desired not to hasten the resumption of my duties before my health is perfectly re-established. I am authorized by my surgeon to entertain hopes of being able to appear before the public on Monday, if it be not in a character requiring too great bodily exertion. With that view I take the liberty of suggesting that of Shylock.

" ' I beg to assure you that I feel convinced that anxiety and impatience of confinement will tend more to delay my perfect recovery from my accident than any ill that may result from too early exertion.

" ' I am, sirs,

" ' Your obedient servant,

" ' E. KEAN.' "

It was probable the public heard rumours of the real cause of his absence, and suspected the statements made regarding his illness. On the night of his re-appearance the theatre was crowded to excess; for some reason the rising of the curtain was delayed, and the audience, already in a state of excitement, became impatient. When at last the play began, a general cry arose of "Off, off, Kean, Kean, apology." After speaking some of his lines, not one word of which was heard, Rae, who represented Bassanio, bowed and quitted the stage, followed by Antonio. At that moment a distraction was caused by the entrance of the Duke of Gloucester and the Princess Sophia, when *God save the King* was demanded by the gallery, and responded to by the orchestra. Some of the performers coming forward were soundly hissed, until it was discovered their intention was to sing "the loyal hymn," when they were listened to with approval. Having finished, they retired, and for some seconds the audience waited in complete silence, expecting Kean to appear and apologize; but in this they were disappointed, for Bassanio and Antonio came on, and again began their parts.

Dire confusion followed. Shouts of "Off, off," were mingled with cries of "Go on," "Apology," and "No apology." In the midst of this excitement the attention of the house was directed to a box in which the occupants were engaged in active dispute, presumably with reference to Kean. Threats and words of anger were interchanged, and this diverting the audience from its own grievance, the play was allowed to proceed uninterruptedly until Kean entered as Shylock. Then arose cries for an apology, and counter cries of " No apology!" and the air was noisy with hisses and cheers. Cool and collected, Kean began his part in the midst of this violent uproar, no one word he spoke being heard, until, after the elapse of some minutes, during which the storm seemed to increase, he removed his hat, and advanced to the front of the stage. Then silence falling upon all, he spoke as follows—

" It is the first time in my life that I have been the unwilling cause of disappointment. That in this theatre it is the first instance out of the hundred and sixty-nine performances, I appeal to your own recollection and to the testimony of the managers. It is to your favour I owe whatever reputation I enjoy. It is upon your candour I throw myself when prejudice would deprive me of what you have bestowed."

This speech, which contained no word of excuse, was interrupted by bursts of applause, and received with ringing cheers. He then continued his represent-ation, and never did he play Shylock better than on this evening, nor did he ever receive warmer appreciation.

At the close of the season 1816 Kean was presented with a silver cup, modelled after the well-known Warwick vase. For this three hundred guineas had been subscribed by the committee and the company, both men and women, with the exception of Munden and Dowton—the former being remarkable for his penurious spirit, the latter equally notable for his jealousy of Kean. When Munden was asked for his contribution, he replied, "You may cup Mr. Kean if you like, but you don't bleed Joe Munden." The cup, which was adorned with the heads of Shakespeare and Massinger, and with masks of tragedy and comedy, bore the following words—

" To Edmund Kean this vase was presented on the 25th day of June, 1816, by Robert Palmer, father of the Drury Lane company, in the names of Right Hon. Lord Byron, Hon. Douglas Kinnaird, Right Hon. George Lamb, Chandos Leigh, Esq., S. Davies, Esq. (then followed the names of the company, fifty-two in number), in testimony of their admiration of his transcendent talents, and more especially to commemorate his first representation of the character of Sir Giles Overreach on the 12th of January, 1816, when, in common with an astonished public, overcome with the irresistible power of his genius, they received a lasting impression of excellence, which twenty-six successive representations have served but to confirm."

The suicide of Mr. Whitbread in July, 1815, and the departure of Lord Byron from England early in the following year, removed from Kean two friends who had sought to win him from habits which eventually ruined his life. His fondness for drink became stronger with time, and already gave him warning of its effect upon his health; for Grattan narrates, that in the year 1817, seeking him one night when he had played Othello, he found the tragedian in his dressing-room "as usual, after the performance of any of his parts, stretched on a sofa, vomiting violently and throwing up quantities of blood. His face was half-washed, one side deadly pale, the other deep copper colour. He was a very appalling object certainly, even to those who were accustomed to see him."

One of the taverns to which he frequently resorted was kept by Higman, a bass singer, who, in the sere and yellow leaf of his days, had abandoned his calling to become the proprietor of a public-house in Villiers Street, the sign of which he changed to that of Richard III. Higman's friends—fiddlers and actors, singers and musicians—came here at night when the play-houses and the concert-halls closed; and many a pleasant story of famous comedians and tragedians dead and gone, and many a merry anecdote of comrades yet alive and strolling, was told. It happened one night that Kean entered the tavern, when a ventriloquist and mimic named Fuller had begun a series of imitations of famous actors, which a programme announced included Bannister, Young, Kemble, and Kean.

Fuller had frequently mimicked other actors in Kean's presence, but had never ventured to imitate the great tragedian to his face. Kean quietly seated himself, listened with amusement, and occasionally tapped the table by way of approbation. Then came the moment for the imitation of Kean. Fuller paused and looked at him, but apparently he assented to the performance, and the mimic began a speech of Richard III. in his manner. But scarce had he repeated five lines when Kean flung a glass of wine in his face. Instantly a scuffle followed, the would-be combatants were separated, and Kean, with eyes flaming, swore, if he thought he was such a wretch as Fuller represented he would hang himself. Like all distinguished men, he was plagued with a host of human gnats styling themselves imitators —men who produced some poor semblance to his mannerisms without being able to give any idea of his powers, and of such was Fuller.

With a country actor named Anderton he was more tolerant. Whilst Kean was spending an evening at the Harp tavern, Anderton, accompanied by some provincial players, entered. Having acted with Kean in by-gone days he now addressed him, but the tragedian either did not hear or remember him. The frequenters of the Harp were generally known as the Screaming Lunatics, and in order to make good their claim to this title, all new comers were expected to sing or recite. When Anderton's turn came to pay his footing, he gave imitations of well-known actors. He had gained considerable reputation by recitations after the manner of Kean, but withheld them on the present occasion. His friends, however, were not satisfied by the omission, and cried out, " Give us Kean ; let us have Kean ;" and Anderton rose, and complied with the request. There were those present who remembered the scene with Fuller, and now expected a repetition of the occurrence, and one of Kean's friends rose up, declaring he would not sit by and hear the greatest living genius mimicked by a mountebank. Kean's reply was a glance of contempt, then turning to his imitator, said, " Anderton, I didn't know you," on which they shook hands heartily, and spent the night in each other's company.

Kean was one of the last men to forget the friends and acquaintance he had met in the days of poverty and distress, as many instances show. Here also is a letter written in May, 1817, which speaks for him on this point—

"DEAR BRIDGE,

"I did not see you yesterday in New Street, or should immediately have spoken. You know little of me if you think it necessary to apologize for breach of ceremony—all the fashionable parade of 'card leaving,' 'at home,' 'the honour of your company,' &c., I have long since, with the rubbish appertaining to it, kicked out of my doors. The friends with whom I wish to associate are such as will come uninvited, go unretarded, share the family meal, drink half-a-dozen bottles if he can, a pint if it better suits his inclinations, laugh at the follies of the world, pity those poor devils in the shackles of refinement, chatter philosophy, and sing a good song—if these are the ingredients that form a man worthy of J. B. Bridge's consideration, there is none will be more happy to take him by the hand than his

"Very sincere friend,
"EDMUND KEAN.

" P.S.—·When I am not at home I am at the theatre, and theatre or home, drop in when you please."

When he had played at Exeter, it had been his habit to meet some boon companions in a certain room in the Turk's Head tavern almost every evening. He had left that town depressed by poverty and misery, and had not visited it until the summer of 1816, when he went to perform for a few nights at the theatre. As his carriage and four entered Exeter, he ordered it should be driven straight to the Turk's Head, and as it arrived at the inn the great actor quietly descended, ran along a familiar passage, opened the door of a well-known room, and with a spring, jumped on a table surrounded by his old companions, crying, " Richard's himself again."

His remembrance of good fellowship is proved by another story which Tom Conningham was proud to tell. Kean and he had been strollers poor in one company, and had shared together the trials and privations common to their state. But whilst Kean had risen in the world, Conningham remained in distress. Soon after Kean's fame had been established, Tom was playing at Brighton, and on the occasion of his benefit a fellow-player suggested he should ask his old friend to act for him, when a full house would certainly be secured, and Tom's debts swept into oblivion.

"My good fellow," quoth honest Tom, "I should be afraid to make so bold a request. It is true we were at one time acting together, and he was then a good-natured man; but Ned Kean the stroller and Edmund Kean the prop of Drury Lane are different persons."

His adviser argued that change of fortune need not necessarily rob a man of his better nature, and eventually persuaded him to write to the tragedian. In reply he received the following letter—

"DEAR TOM,

"I am sorry you are not so comfortable in life as you could wish. Put me up for any of my plays next Thursday, and I shall be happy to act for your benefit. In the mean time, accept the enclosed trifle to make the pot boil.

"Yours truly,

"EDMUND KEAN."

The enclosure was a ten-pound note. On the day named he arrived at Brighton, and played to a great house, the receipts of which enabled Conningham to begin life as a free man.

A few years later he paid a visit to Northallerton for three nights. The terms of agreement were that he was to have half the receipts. The prices of admission were doubled, but for all that the theatre was crowded to excess. The morning after the first performance, the proprietor, Samuel Butler, called on Kean to give him forty pounds, his share of the profits. "Put it in your pocket," said Kean briefly; and then, as the manager looked at him wonderingly, continued, "When I was a stripling in this town your father assisted me to travel to London. At parting I told him, if ever fortune smiled on me I would not forget him. Fortune has smiled on me, and I am proud of paying to the son the debt so many years due to the father. Put up your money, and then we shall proceed according to the terms of our engagement."

On another occasion he played for the benefit of manager Moss, in whose company he had served when Moss was a prosperous man, but whom he now found in sickness and poverty. And again, when he had played for three nights at Totnes, he came forward at the conclusion of his performance and said—"Ladies and Gentlemen, My engagement is over, but I stay one night more to act gratis for the manager's benefit; for when I was only a stroller he helped me in my distress, and now that I can perhaps help him, I will willingly do so."

Numerous appeals were made to him for help by those he had formerly known, nor was application ever made in vain; for his purse was ever open to relieve distress. Having once given a suit of clothes and money to a young actor, and subsequently obtained for him a three years' engagement at a London theatre, he gave his reasons for his deeds. "He was at Richmond," he said, "when I walked down to play there for one night. I was to have ten shillings for acting, and the rehearsal was to begin at ten. I sat up all night at the Harp, for I had no lodgings, and started at six in the morning. About nine o'clock I was crossing Richmond Green, when he saw and invited me to breakfast. I was terribly hungry, and hadn't a halfpenny about me. I breakfasted and dined with him, acted like a Trojan, and then walked back to London with my earnings, minus a parting glass. I shall never forget the invitation or the inviter."

But if he recollected favours done him in his youth, he likewise remembered insults offered him. Whenever in the course of the summer months he visited Taunton to appear as a star at its theatre, nothing could induce him to behave with friendliness towards the manager, who every night duly brought him half the receipts of the house as the salary he had agreed to pay him; but no sooner did Kean hear his well-known knock at the dressing-room door, than he invariably called aloud to his dresser, "See what that man wants." In the course of a few years, Kean, in visiting Taunton, found this individual stricken by losses; the theatre had passed from his possession, his services as an actor had been rejected, and he was steeped in poverty. In this state he called upon Kean, and begged he would play one night for his benefit; and to this the tragedian assented.

That evening, as Kean and some actors sat in the public room of a tavern, telling anecdotes concerning their fellows, and drinking convivial glasses, they were joined by the ex-manager, who, believing Kean's dislike for him had vanished, presently rose and made a speech, in which he stated, that the great actor having known and served under him in the period of his prosperity, had generously consented to play for him now in the days of his adversity. In the midst of loud acclamations which followed Kean stood up, and the light in his eyes and pallor of his face caused sudden silence. Turning to the speaker, he said in cold and measured tones, "Don't let us misunderstand one another. I am bound to you by no ties from my former acquaintance. I don't play for you because you were once my manager, or a manager, for if ever a man deserved his fate it is you ; if ever there was a family of tyrants it is yours. I don't play for you from former friendship, but I play because you are a fallen man." The effect of this speech was electrical ; but he to whom it was addressed overlooked the affront in consideration of the promised help, and soon after left the room. Then Kean, from whom all anger had departed, said to those present, "I am sorry I forgot myself, but when I and my family were starving, that fellow refused to let a subscription for me be entertained in his theatre."

Another anecdote illustrating his remembrance of injuries is stated in the *Theatrical Magazine.* Having one morning, whilst visiting Portsmouth, finished a rehearsal at the theatre, the manager asked him to come and drink a bottle of Madeira at a neighbouring inn. Nothing loath, the tragedian went, and the proprietor learning the name of his distinguished customer, attended him personally, ushered him into his best room, and thanked him for the honour of his visit, with many gracious words and formal bows. Kean without replying fixed his eyes on him, knit his brows, and after some time said, "I came into your house at the request of this gentleman to have some refreshments, not to be pestered with your civilities, which to me are so many insults. Look at me well, sir; you don't recollect me, I see, but I am the same Edmund Kean I was fifteen years ago, when you kept a small tavern in this town. At that time I was a strolling player, and came with my company to a fair here. I remember well that I went one day into the bar of your house, and called for a half-pint of porter, which, after I had waited your pleasure patiently, was held out to me by you with one hand, whilst the other was extended to receive the money. Never shall I forget your insolent demeanour, or the bitterness of my feelings. What alteration beyond that of dress do you find in me? Am I a better man than I was then? What is there in me now that should cause you to overwhelm me with compliments? Go, keep your wine in your cellar, I'll have none of it," and so saying, he turned his back upon the landlord and left his house, followed by the manager.

But the adventures of the day were not yet ended. No sooner had they left the inn than Kean, addressing his friend, said, " Now I will take you to an honest fellow who was kind to me in the days of my misfortune, and walking down the street, they entered a dark-looking little tavern, where they seated themselves at a side-table, called for some wine, and at the same time expressed a desire to see the landlord.   He came, and bowed; but he was not the host of the tragedian's recollections, for he had departed with past years. There happened, however, to be a waiter in the house who had served the strolling player, and with him Kean talked, making inquiries of his late master's family, and of old frequenters of the tavern, known to both.   After some time Kean said he must go, and asked the man what was the time.   "I'll see, sir," he replied, running to the stairs, at the head of which stood an old case clock.   On his return, Kean asked him if he had not got a watch.   He replied he had not.

"Then take this," said Kean, "and buy one; and whenever you look at it, think of your late master."

He handed him a five-pound note, which the man received without a word, surprise and gratitude rendering him mute.

CHAPTER IX.

IN the winter season of 1816, a new sensation was caused in the theatrical world by the first appearance of William Macready at Covent Garden Theatre. This famous actor was born in Tottenham Court Road, London, in March, 1793, and was therefore six years younger than Edmund Kean. His father had begun life in Dublin as an upholsterer, but had eventually become a player, and finally manager of the Manchester, Birmingham, Sheffield, and Newcastle theatres. Macready the elder was a bustling, sharp-tempered, sanguine-spirited little man, whose ambition it was to have one of his sons at the Bar, and one in the army. William Charles, his eldest born, was destined for the law, and at an early age was sent to Rugby school, where he remained three years.

At the end of that period the elder Macready fell into difficulties, and eventually his affairs became desperate. His son, who had not yet reached his sixteenth birthday, was at this time home in Manchester for the holidays, and seeing the condition of his father's prospects, resolved to help him so far as in him lay. Therefore he one day told his father he would not return to Rugby, as he wished to become a player. The manager replied, it had been the desire of his life to see his boy a barrister, but if he wished to go on the stage, he would not oppose his desires. Accordingly young Macready promptly and steadily prepared himself for his · calling—learning to fence, studying parts suited to his powers, and watching the effects produced by various actors.

As time passed the manager's troubles increased, until, living in great fear of being arrested for debt, he was obliged to hide from the bailiffs, and leave his son to represent him at the theatre. Eventually he surrendered himself to the sheriff's officer, and was lodged in Lancaster Castle. When his son found him really a prisoner, his fortitude gave way, and he burst into tears, on which his father grimly said, "There is nothing I cannot bear but compassion; if you cannot command yourself, go away." He was then sent to take charge of a company of players in his father's service at Chester; reaching which town, the lad found them in a state of mutiny, because their salaries were in arrears, and indifferent as to how they acted. This the manager of sixteen summers undertook to rectify, by insisting on careful rehearsals, and the repetition of the proper text. Moreover, he introduced a new play, exerted himself to obtain " bespeaks " from rival political candidates, and succeeded in drawing full houses nightly. Working in this manner, he was enabled to pay most of the debts connected with the theatre, and was gradually prospering, when the landlord of the house put in an execution for rent due. Sadly perplexed, he wrote to some friends, requesting they would lend him what money they could spare, and they complying, he was enabled to defray all debts and pay all salaries.

And having closed the theatre at Chester, he, with three of the best actors of his company, set out for Newcastle-on-Tyne, having barely sufficient money in his pocket to pay travelling expenses. It was Christmas

Eve when they started in a chaise, and journeying all
through a bitterly cold night, reached Brough, a small
town on the borders of Westmoreland, about noon on
Christmas Day. Here they stayed to have lunch, having
eaten which Macready tendered a five-pound note to
the waiter, but was soon amazed to find his host come
bustling into the room, declaring he did not like the
look of this piece of paper, and would have nought to
do with it. Knowing that unless the note was changed
he could not pay the post-boy who had driven him, or
get fresh horses to take him on his way, Macready was
sorely perplexed. Moreover, his hopes of being able to
return the money he had recently borrowed, and of opening the Christmas season well at the Newcastle Theatre,
of which his father was still lessee, depended on his
reaching that town by Boxing Day. This consummation
the landlord's suspicions threatened to prevent. The
young manager had already left his watch at Chester,
that he might raise funds to defray the expenses of his
journey, and had no other money save the note. After
a whispered consultation with his three companions,
they offered their watches to the landlord, on condition
that he would advance three pounds on them, and give
change for the note; to which, after some hesitation, he
consented, but stipulated, as the roads were bad, they

should have four horses to carry them forward. Glad of escape from threatened captivity, even on these conditions, they agreed to his wishes, and presently galloping away from the crowd which had gathered round the inn to witness their departure, they gave three ringing cheers by way of venting their feelings and raising their spirits.

Arrived at Newcastle, Macready produced a pantomime founded on the tragedy of *Macbeth*, which met with success. During the first representation of this piece an unrehearsed incident took place. At the end of the first scene, when Macbeth and his lady had dyed their hands in innocent blood, they were supposed to make their exits, wash their hands, and reappear stainless three minutes later in the next scene. But it happened when Macbeth left the stage, the dresser, who should have attended with water, soap, and towel, was conspicuous by his absence, being indeed waiting at the opposite wings, where he was not wanted. Poor Macbeth stamped with rage, and swore round oaths, on which Macready rushed to his aid, and dragging him to the nearest dressing-room, offered him a jug of water, in which the murderer dipped his hands, and then catching something which bore semblance to a cloth, presented it as a towel. Having left the impressions of his gory fingers on this article, Macbeth rushed back to the boards. The manager, yet with the jug of water and improvised towel in his hands, was crossing the back of the stage, when he encountered Lady Macbeth in search of her dresser, and to her he likewise offered the aid of that which had already served her spouse; and she having washed herself clean, Macready left the cloth and jug in his own room.

The pantomime caused great laughter and gained much applause, so that Macready, going home that night in a shower of blinding snow, felt gratified for his success. But next morning the acting manager met him with a very grave face, and stated he was sorry to tell him there were thieves in the theatre.

"Good heavens! is it possible?" asked Macready. "What has been stolen?"

"Well, Mr. Simkins's breeches are missing," the other replied. "When at the end of the evening he went to dress they were gone, and he was obliged to walk home through the snow in a kilt."

Macready gave directions that strict search and inquiry should be made, and no pains spared to detect the offender; but scarce had he uttered these words, when it occurred to him that the improvised towel must have been the missing garment, and hastening to his room, he there found the breeches streaked with crimson dye.

Under his direction the theatre prospered, so that he was enabled to send his father three pounds weekly for his support until his release from prison. At the close of the season the company went to Birmingham, where the elder Macready resumed his occupation as manager. And now the project of his son's appearance on the stage, deferred in consequence of his labours, was resumed. The character of Romeo was selected for his *début*, and the lad, now in his seventeenth year, began to study the part with great earnestness. His hopes of success were not raised by the occasional remarks of his father, who declared his attempts "would never do;" though they were upheld by the stout matron who was to be his Juliet. On Thursday, June 7th, 1810, the play-bills announced that "the tragedy of *Romeo and Juliet*, written by Shakespeare," would be performed, "the part of Romeo by a young gentleman, being his first appearance upon any stage." The house was crowded, the curtain rose, and presently the new Romeo appeared. Of his sensations he wrote, "The emotions I experienced on first crossing the stage, and coming forward in face of the lights and the applauding audience, were almost overpowering. There was a mist before my eyes. I seemed to see nothing of the dazzling scene before me, and for some time I was like an automaton, moving on certain defined limits. I went mechanically through the variations in which I had drilled myself, and it was not until the plaudits of the audience woke me from the kind of waking dream in which I seemed to be moving, that I gained my self-possession, and really entered into the spirit of the character, and, I may say, felt the passion I was to represent. Every round of applause acted like inspiration on me; I 'trod on air,' became another being, or a happier self; and when the curtain fell at the conclusion of the play, and the intimate friends and performers crowded on the stage to raise up the Juliet and myself, shaking my hands with fervent congratulations, a lady asked me, 'Well, sir; how do you feel now?' my boyish answer was, without disguise, 'I feel as if I should like to act it all over again.' "

The sense and judgment he had already proved himself to possess, showed him, that instead of placing faith in the impartial criticisms and favourable opinions of his friends, and of his father's company, he must work hard if he would finally triumph. Therefore he studied new parts, thought over the possible effects they admitted, sought to correct such defects as he was conscious of, and on Sundays, when the theatre was free from the presence of all *employées*, he was wont to lock himself in, pace the stage to give himself ease, and make himself familiar with the entrances and exits, and recite his speeches, until, weary and exhausted, he was glad to breathe fresh air again. This practice he continued for years.

Gradually he came to represent leading parts in the plays produced at his father's theatre, and whilst at Newcastle had the honour of acting with the great Mrs. Siddons, who played here for two nights, whilst on her way to give a series of farewell performances at Edinburgh. When he learned that he was to appear with her in the same cast, his fears were great; and the hour when he was to rehearse with her at the Queen's Head Hotel, was one filled with dread for him. Coming for the first time into the command-ing presence of the queen of tragedy, her stateliness and gravity filled him with awe; indeed, his nervous-ness was so considerable, that she smilingly remarked, "I hope, Mr. Macready, you have brought some harts-horn and water with you, as I am told you are terribly frightened at me."

This remark did not aid him in gaining his self-possession, and his terror increased as the time

approached for him to play the part of her husband
in the tragedy of *The Gamester*. At last the curtain
rose, and his worst anticipations seemed about to be
fulfilled; fear seized him, presence of mind forsook
him, memory vanished, and he stood motionless on
the stage, until she approached and whispered the
words of his part; then the scene proceeded. By
degrees he recovered, until in the last act he had the
gratification of hearing her say, as she stood at the
wings, "Bravo, sir, bravo!" and her praise was echoed
by the audience. On the second night he played
young Norval to her Lady Randolph, and succeeded
more to his satisfaction. During his brief acquaintance
with the great actress he secured her interest, and in
parting she gave him advice, which all aspirants for
fame might fitly take to heart. "You are in the right
way," she said kindly; "but remember what I say,
study, study, study, and do not marry till you are
thirty. I remember what it was to be obliged to study,
at nearly your age, with a young family about me.
Beware of that; keep your mind on your art; do not
remit your study, and you are certain to succeed. Do
not forget my words, study well, and God bless you."

This counsel lived with him, and in those moments
of dark despondency to which all sensitive minds are

subjected it cheered him on his way. Through unremitting study and continual practise he strengthened his talents and increased his fame, until at last, in December 1814, he accepted an engagement to play at Bath. On arriving by coach at this ancient city, his heart fluttered on seeing his name announced in big letters on the play-bills; and the same sight awakened a nervous emotion in him so long as he remained a player. "I have often crossed over to the other side of the street," he writes, "to avoid passing by a play-bill in which my name might be figuring." This ancient city was then a place of favourite resort. Women of fashion, men of wealth, soldiers and politicians, youths from the universities, maidens fresh in the matrimonial market, crowded the hotels and boarding-houses, gathered in the pump-rooms at mid-day to drink the waters and talk scandal, thronged Harrison's Gardens at noon to flirt and enjoy wit, filled the assembly rooms on Wednesday and Friday evenings, patronized concerts on Tuesday evenings, and assembled in brilliant array at the theatre on Saturday nights.

The favourable judgment of such audiences was considered a safe passport for actors to the great London playhouses, aware of which, Macready looked forward with apprehension to his first appearance before them. A great and fashionable crowd gathered to witness his Romeo, and the reception which greeted him strung his efforts to the highest pitch. As he proceeded the applause increased, until in the scene with Tybalt it swelled into prolonged cheering, and the curtain fell upon an assured triumph. Leaving the theatre elated by success, and hopeful of future fame, Macready hastened to his lodgings in Chapel Row, Queen Square, that he might immediately write and post the joyful news of his success to his family.

His manager rejoiced exceedingly, the public lauded him, and the press, with a solitary exception, commended him. The dissenting critic regretted that the young man could never be a great actor, because of his want of personal attractions, "by which," this individual eloquently expressed himself, "nature had interposed an everlasting barrier to his success." Later, the same gifted writer assured his readers, Macready's personation of Beverley in *The Gamesters* would have been altogether excellent "but for the unaccommodating disposition of nature in the formation of his face." In height Macready was five feet seven inches, his hair was light, his eyes blue, and his face, though flat and heavy in repose, was capable of great expression in moments of feeling and excitement.

His performance of Romeo was followed by representations of Hamlet, Richard III., Orestes, and Norval, and the sensation he created gradually spreading to London, Fawcett, the stage-manager of Covent Garden Theatre, was sent to see and report on his acting. Favourably impressed, he waited on Macready, and inquired of him what were his views regarding a London engagement; to which the latter replied, he would not hazard an appearance in the capital except upon a high salary, and for a term of years; as, if he were not successful in winning public favour at first, he would have a chance of gaining it later; and if he were not able to secure it eventually, he should be indemnified for the loss of the estimation he at present enjoyed in the provinces.

The stage manager's return to London was followed by the offer of an engagement for three years at Covent Garden, but the salary was not agreed upon. Meanwhile, Macready's season at Bath having concluded, he acted for a couple of nights at Bristol, and then accepted a proposition from the Dublin Theatre to play there for seven weeks, at a salary of fifty pounds per week.

The elder Macready, who was naturally anxious for his son's appearance in town, proposed to Harris, then part proprietor and acting manager of Covent Garden, that the young actor should be engaged for six or eight nights at twenty pounds a night; his permanent stay at the theatre to be determined by the impression he made. Harris readily accepted the suggestion, but on its being laid before him whom it most concerned, he rejected it decisively. He now resolved to spend another year in the provinces before trying his strength in town. Having played at Glasgow, he crossed over to Dublin, where he acted his principal characters to appreciative houses. Whilst here he was much struck by the attention, sensitiveness, and sympathy of his audiences, and greatly diverted by their humour. Of this last trait he had heard many anecdotes, especially one, which amused him greatly, concerning a tragedian named Laurence Clinch, an old favourite of the citizens. It happened one night when Clinch acted Othello by command of the Lord-Lieutenant, a brilliant house assembled to witness his performance. In due time Clinch made his first entry, when, on turning his back, it was evident the tragedian had not noticed some slight disarrangement in his dress, which caused a general titter that soon developed into a roar of laughter, when one of his admirers, in a state of great excitement, leaned over the gallery, and putting his hand to his mouth, as if he would whisper his remarks to the actor's ear, called out, "Larry, honey, there's the smallest taste in life of your shirt got out behind you."

Macready was fortunate enough to hear for himself a specimen of Hibernian humour. During a performance of *Venice Preserved* one evening, the actor who represented Jaffier drawled his speeches to uncommon length. In the last act, where he struck himself with a dagger, he droned out a soliloquy which was heard with evident impatience, until at last an impetuous god cried out, "Arrah, die at once;" to which one of his fellows from the opposite side responded, "Be quiet, you blackguard;" and then turning to the expiring Jaffier, said in a patronizing tone, "Sure, take your time," remarks which spoiled the fine effects of the tragedian.

Whilst in Dublin negotiations were again made for Macready's appearance at Covent Garden and at Drury Lane, but the committee of the latter theatre, thinking his terms extravagant, abandoned the idea of engaging him; whilst Fawcett wrote, "Kean seems likely to be more in your way at Drury Lane than Young would be at Covent Garden. All your best parts you might act with us, and not trespass upon anybody. Come to us next year—for one year, two years, three years, or for life. The article shall be made as you please, only don't be exorbitant." Macready felt that a London engagement, the zenith of every actor's ambition, would be to him a hazardous step; for already he was held in repute in the provinces, and drew good salaries, advantages he would certainly lose if he failed to gain the favour of London audiences. However, after much consideration, he required and received a contract from the lessee of Covent Garden, whereby he was engaged to become a member of the company of that theatre for five years, at the rate of sixteen pounds a week for two years, seventeen pounds a week for the following two years, and eighteen pounds a week for the last year.

Before leaving Dublin he witnessed the remarkable performance of an amateur named Plunkett, in the character of Richard III. Mr. Plunkett was a barrister unknown to briefs, and was closely related to Lord Fingall; his harmless eccentricities, amongst which was strong faith in his dramatic abilities, rendered him dear to the Dublin public, who mercifully regarded his inordinate vanity as mental weakness. On this occasion he, as the bills stated, " appeared before the public for the purpose of giving him a claim at a future period for a benefit in order to relieve the distressed port of Dublin and its vicinity." Great were the expectations of merriment which his performance promised, and the evening on which he trod the boards saw the theatre crowded to excess. Applause and laughter greeted him, and as he proceeded the wits in the pit and gallery joined in the dialogue, to the vast delight of the house. When he declared "I can smile, and murder while I smile," a voice quickly responded, "Oh, be the powers you can;" and to his question, "Am I then a man to be beloved?" a chorus answered, "Indeed then, you're not." His manner of delivering the phrase, "Off with his head," was ironically encored, and at his death the theatre was in a general uproar of mock approbation, derisive cheering, and hearty laughter. But Plunkett took the storm to indicate applause, and next morning called on Lord Chief Justice Bushe to hear his opinion of the performance; and on his lordship expressing his regret that he had been unable to visit the theatre, the distinguished amateur insisted on reciting some of Richard's speeches, notwithstanding the protest of the Chief Justice, who feared the gathering of a mob about his windows. When he had finished he pressed for an opinion from his lordship, who declared, "He had never seen anything like it in all the performances he had ever witnessed," a sentence which Plunkett had inserted in all the papers next day as the veritable judgment pronounced on his acting by the Chief Justice.

Macready's self-confidence had never been great, and as the time approached for him to make his appearance before a London audience, his nervousness increased. Shrinking from the ordeal, he would willingly have deferred it until his talents were more matured, his experiences wider; but this being impossible, he, with fear and hope contending for supremacy, prepared for the trial on which his future career must depend. Arriving in London in September, 1816, he put up at the old Slaughter Coffee House, and duly presented himself to Harris of Covent Garden Theatre, who, with Fawcett and Fred Reynolds, sat in council to determine in which character he should first appear. "A club much talked of at that time," says Macready, "that bore the name of the Wolves, was said to be banded together to put down any one appearing in Kean's characters. I believe the report not to be founded on strict fact; but it was currently received, and had its influence on the Covent Garden deliberations." It was finally decided he should appear as Orestes in the *Distressed Mother*, on Monday the 16th instant.

The long-expected day at length arrived, and after an early dinner, Macready lay down to rest and compose himself until the hour came for his departure to the theatre. Then he entered a hackney coach, which to his excited imagination seemed as a hurdle conveying him to execution. Reaching the play-house, he dressed in silence, only interrupted by the dread voice of the call-boy announcing " Overture on, sir," and presently summoning him, when, with a firm step, he went forward to his trial. " The appearance of resolute composure assumed by the player at this turning-point of his life belies the internal struggles he endures," writes Macready, describing this hour. " These eventful trials, in respect to the state of mind and body in which they are encountered, so resemble each other, that one described describes all. The same agitation, and effort to master it, the dazzled vision, the short, quick breath, the dry palate, the throbbing of the heart —all, however painfully felt, must be effectually disguised in the character the actor strives to place before his audience."

Abbott, who was to play Pylades, waited for him at the wings, and when the curtain had risen Macready grasped his hand, and dashing on the stage, exclaiming as in a transport of joy, " Oh, Pylades, what's life without a friend ? " A loud burst of applause from a crowded house, which numbered many distinguished men,

amcngst whom was Edmund Kean, greeted his appearance; but it was not until the loud plaudits which
followed his passionate utterance of the line, "Oh, ye
gods, give me Hermione, or let me die," that he
recovered his self-possession. As the play proceeded
he became more and more animated under the conflict-
ing emotions of the distracted lover, and at its close
the prolonged cheers of his audience assured him of
success.

Congratulations were heartily offered him by the
company as he passed, panting with excitement, to his
dressing-room; the play was given out for repetition on
the following Friday and Monday; and Harris, having
summoned him to his presence, exclaimed, " Well, my
boy, you have done capitally, and if you could carry a
play along with such a cast, I don't know what you
cannot do." Macready returned to his lodgings "in a
state of mind like one not fully awake from a disturbing
dream, grateful for my escape, yet almost questioning
the reality of what had passed." That night sleep
deserted his excited mind, and he anxiously waited the
hour when he might read the criticisms on his performance in the morning papers. Taken generally, they
were laudatory. The *Times* was kind enough to allow
him "a certain amount of ability," but not sufficient to

shake Young, or intimidate Charles Kemble; the *Globe* was certain he was "a man of mind," and noticed that the sparks of his genius frequently kindled to a blaze; whilst Hazlitt in the *Examiner* had not the slightest hesitation in saying Macready was "by far the best tragic actor that had come out in his remembrance with the exception of Mr. Kean." Unfavourable comments on his personal appearance were freely made. "He is not handsome in face or person," said the *Times;* the *Globe* considered tragedy required "features of a more prominent and strongly-marked description than those which he possesses." His eyes were admitted by that organ to be full of fire, "and when in the paroxysm we mark their wild transitions, our attention is entirely withdrawn from the flatness of the features they irradiate;" but the *News* honestly declared he was "the plainest and most awkwardly made man that ever trod the stage."

It was sufficiently unpleasant for Macready to read such descriptions of his person, but perhaps it was yet more irritating for him to overhear the remarks of his neighbours regarding himself, as he sat one evening in the second tier of boxes at the theatre.

"Have you seen the new actor?" asked a lady of her companion.

"What, Macready," he replied, unconscious that the subject of their conversation was at hand. "No, I've not seen him yet; I'm told he is a capital actor, but a devilish ugly fellow."

To crown all, he heard that Charles Kemble said to his brother John, he was sure Macready would gain the highest rank in his profession, to which John Kemble, who owed so much of his success to his personal appearance, replied, "Oh, Charles, with that face!"

Macready, unfortunately, could not boast of advantages such as generally help to establish other actors in public favour. He is minutely described by James Henry Hackett, as being "above the middle height, his port rather stiffly erect, his figure not stout, but very straight, and at the hips quite the reverse of *embonpoint*. His ordinary or natural gait is not dignified, he steps short and quick, with a springy action of the knee-joints, which, sometimes trundling his stiff bust—as in a rush from the centre to the corner of the stage—reminds one of the recoil of a cannon upon its carriage. In his slow and measured tread of the stage he seems somewhat affected; he sways his body alternately on either leg, whilst his head waves from side to side to balance it."

The second play in which he appeared was a dull tragedy called *The Italian Lover*, in which, though he was recognized as " a various and skilful painter of the human passions," he created little attention. As this representation brought no profit to the treasury, the manager, in a moment of impatience, decided that he should appear as Othello and Iago alternately with Charles Young. This was a movement Macready felt to be injudicious. Kean's Othello was yet fresh in the public mind, and all comparisons with such a performance as his must prove unfavourable; moreover, Othello was a character he had seldom played, whilst he had never either studied or acted Iago. Remonstrance with Harris proved useless, and Macready appeared as the Moor and his Ancient without success. Hazlitt described Young in Othello as being like a great humming-top, and Macready as Iago, like a mischievous boy whipping him.

In October Miss O'Neill returned to Covent Garden from the provinces, and before her all other attractions paled. About the same time John Philip Kemble caused great interest amongst his admirers, by announcing his last season, before taking his farewell of the stage. Macready now regretted he had not delayed making appearance in town for another year. To

Young was given the leading tragic parts, whilst the heroes of comedy were allotted to Charles Kemble. Little scope was therefore given him for the display of talents which it was admitted he possessed, and he greatly feared he might dwindle down to the dread level of mediocrity, known to the profession as respectable. An event soon occurred which increased his fears.

END OF VOL. I.

i

ii

COURT LIFE BELOW STAIRS;

OR,

LONDON UNDER THE LAST GEORGES.

By J. FITZGERALD MOLLOY,

AUTHOR OF "ROYALTY RESTORED."

Crown 8vo., 6s.

"These volumes must be regarded as a valuable contribution to literature; presenting as they do a series of clever, graphic and reliable pictures of the court and social life under the last Georges."—*Sunday Times.*

"Mr. Molloy's style is crisp, and carries the reader along; his portraits of the famous men and women of the time are etched with care, and his narrative rises to intensity and dramatic impressiveness as he follows the latter days of Queen Caroline."—*British Quarterly Review.*

"Mr. Molloy's style is bright and fluent, picturesque and animated, and he tells his story with unquestionable skill and vivacity."—*Athenæum.*

"The narrative is fluent and amusing, and is far more instructive than nine-tenths of the novels published nowadays."—*St. James's Gazette.*

"Mr. Molloy's narrative is concise, and exhibits a wide acquaintance with the men and manners of the age. The anecdotes of the famous men of fashion, wits, fools, or knaves introduced are amusing, and several not generally known enliven the pages."—*Morning Post.*

"Well written, full of facts bearing on every subject under consideration, and abounding with anecdotes of gay and witty debauchees."—*Daily Telegraph.*

"What Pepys has done for the Stuarts, Mr. Molloy has done for their Hanoverian successors. This result of his arduous investigations is one of the most interesting works which has ever come under our notice. It is impossible to open the books at any part without feeling an overpowering desire to continue the perusal."—*Newcastle Chronicle.*

FAMOUS PLAYS.

Crown 8vo., 6s.

"Mr. Fitzgerald Molloy is an earnest and indefatigable author of books, particularly interesting to students of the History of the Drama."—*Punch.*

"Apart from the value of a record so full and exhaustive, it is an interesting study to watch the play of individuality in each of the different authors during the several stages of his pieces, and not less entertaining to follow the train of events leading up to the actual production in each case. Here of course scope exists for Mr. Molloy to make a very palatable dish of small circumstances, reminiscent of wits and men of parts other than those immediately concerned. In a word, 'Famous Plays' is a well written, lively, and thoroughly satisfactory piece of work, which is most worthy of Mr. Molloy's reputation as a stage historian of research and erudition, and an elegant and scholarly writer."—*Stage.*

"By such as prefer the records of an honourable and artistic past to the reports of a garish and blatant present, this odd rehabilitation of unremembered things will be greatly and carefully treasured."—*Vanity Fair.*

"Gives a good idea of the English drama as it existed at certain well-defined periods of its history. . . . The result is a book of a very interesting character, and one that is likely to be much read."—*St. James's Gazette.*

"The story of each of these pieces is not merely an account of its literary genesis, its dramatic production, and its quality and character from the standpoint of the critic or the manager; it is a delightfully gossipy sketch of life and character, manners, fortunes, and adventures. Mr. Molloy has a wonderful gift of revitalizing the past."—*Irish Times.*

WARD & DOWNEY, Publishers,

12, YORK STREET, COVENT GARDEN, LONDON.

ROYALTY RESTORED;

OR,

LONDON UNDER CHARLES II.

By J. FITZGERALD MOLLOY.

Third Edition, 1 vol., Crown 8vo.

"The most important historical work yet achieved by its author. . . . . It has remained for a picturesque historian to achieve such a work in its entirety and to tell a tale as it has never before been told."—*Daily Telegraph.*

"A series of pictures carefully drawn, well composed, and correct in all details. Mr. Molloy writes pleasantly, and his book is thoroughly entertaining."—*Graphic.*

"Presents us for the first time with a complete description of the social habits of the period."—*Globe.*

"We are quite prepared to recognize in it the brisk and fluent style, the ease of narration, and other qualities of a like nature, which, as was pointed out in this journal, characterized his former books."—*Athenæum.*

"The story of Charles's marriage, of the prodigious dowry, of the young Queen's innocence of the ways of his world, her wrongs, her sufferings, her brief resistance, her long, lamentable acquiescence, her unfailing love, is well told in this book. Whenever, in its pages, we catch sight of Catherine, it is a relief from the vile company that crowds them, the shameless women and the contemptible men on whom 'the fountain of honour' lavished distinctions, which ought from thenceforth to have lost all meaning and attraction for honest folk. The author has studied his subjects with care and industry: he reproduces them either singly or in groups, with vivid and stirring effect; the comedy and the tragedy of the Court-life move side by side in his chapters. . . . . A chapter on the Plague is admirable,—impressive without any fine writing; the description of the Fire is better still. To Mr. Molloy's narrative of the Titus Oates episode striking merit must be accorded; also to the closing chapter of the work with its picture of the hard death of King Charles."—*Spectator.*

"In 'Royalty Restored; or, London under Charles II.' Mr. J. Fitzgerald Molloy makes a remarkable advance beyond his preceding works in style and literary method. His book, which is the best, may very well be the last on the subject. . . . The shrewdness, the cynicism, and the profound egotism of the Merry Monarch are dexterously conveyed in this picture of him, and the book is variously and vividly interesting."—*World.*

"The author of 'Royalty Restored' has never offered the public so graphic, so fascinating, so charming an example of faded lives revivified, and dim scenes revitalized by the magic of the picturesque historic sense."—*Boston Literary World.*

"Mr. Molloy has not confined himself to an account of the King and his courtiers. He has given us a study of London during his reign, taken, as far as possible, from rare and invariably authentic sources. We can easily see that a work such as this, in order to be successful, must be the result of the most careful study and the most untiring diligence in the consultation of diaries, records, memoirs, letters, pamphlets, tracts, and papers left by contemporaries familiar with the Court and the Capital. There can be no doubt that Mr. Molloy's book bears evidence on every page of such study and diligence."—*Glasgow Evening News.*

"In his delineation of Charles, Mr. Molloy is very successful. . . He avoids vivid colouring; yet rouses our interest and sympathy with a skilful hand."—*St. James's Gazette.*

WARD & DOWNEY, Publishers,

12, YORK STREET, COVENT GARDEN, LONDON.